MACPHERSON'S LIGHTHOUSE ADVENTURE

MACPHERSON IS HERE!

Lavinia Derwent's down-at-heel, eternally optimistic young errand-boy finds himself caught up in a wonderful adventure. With his usual good luck—and a bit of help from his friends— Macpherson is given the chance of a free holiday at the seaside. So he sets off with his old seadog of a grandfather and his crochety Aunt Janet for a fortnight of surprises.

He meets an extraordinary collection of old and new friends. Even his dreaded employer, Old Skinflint the grocer, turns up! And Macpherson has one adventure after another—but best of all, he takes a trip to the lighthouse.

Jacket illustration by Val Biro

ABOUT THE AUTHOR

Lavinia Derwent was born in No-Man's-Land on a farm on the Scottish side of the Border, so remote that she knew more animals than human-beings. Her head being full of 'beasts', she made up stories about them, invented a character called TAMMY TROOT and later an island called SULA, full of seals and sea-birds.

When she came to live in the big city of Glasgow she met many human-beings, but none that interested her more than a cheerful boy whom she saw in the street, lugging a heavy message-basket. MACPHERSON! Since then Macpherson has taken the place of 'beasts' in her head. Through him she has had many exciting adventures; and is delighted that so many children also follow his fortunes, sending her letters and drawings about Macpherson, Maisie and the other characters.

Lavinia Derwent has written many children's books. But of all her many characters she has the softest spot for MACPHERSON.

Macpherson's Lighthouse Adventure

Lavinia Derwent

Illustrated by Leslie Smith

KNIGHT BOOKS
Hodder and Stoughton

Printed and bound in Great Britain for
Hodder and Stoughton Paperbacks, a
division of Hodder and Stoughton Ltd.,
Mill Road, Dunton Green, Sevenoaks,
Kent (Editorial Office: 47 Bedford
Square, London, WC1 3DP) by
Richard Clay (The Chaucer Press) Ltd.,
Bungay, Suffolk

ISBN 0 340 23850 X

Contents

Macpherson's
Lighthouse
Adventure

I

Sea View

Macpherson could not believe his luck. Instead of trudging round the Glasgow streets lugging a heavy message-basket, here he was at the seaside. On holiday!

"This is it, Grandpa!" he called out in an excited voice. "I can read the name on the gate. *Sea View*."

"So it is, my hearty," said the old man, gazing at the tumbledown cottage ahead of him. Grandpa, who had sailed the seas in his younger days, always spoke as if he was still aboard ship. "Heave ho, Macpherson! We're at the seaside."

Aunt Janet laid down her suitcase and sniffed. "Sea View! That's a silly name for it. How can we see the sea from here? It's miles away."

They were all hot and tired after their long walk from the station, and Aunt Janet was never in a good mood at the best of times. But Grandpa could always see the bright side.

"Nonsense, Janet woman. I can smell the salt air," he said, taking a great gulp as if he was

swallowing a mouthful of it. "Cheer up. We'
here to enjoy ourselves."

Macpherson was enjoying himself already. He
darted forward to open the rickety gate, then
cried out when it fell off its hinges. "Mercy me!
I hope there are some nails and a hammer in the
house. Oh look! Roses!"

"More weeds than roses," grumbled Aunt
Janet, looking down her nose at the tangle of
flowers and nettles in the untidy garden. But
Macpherson was delighted with it, even though it
looked like a wilderness. At home in their Glasgow
skyscraper they could see neither roses nor weeds
from their windows.

"Come on, Grandpa. Let's go in," he said, and
helped the old man up the path. He took a key
from his pocket, fitted it into the lock and cried,
"Open Sesame!" The door creaked open, and they
were in. "Welcome to Sea View."

It was only a small cottage. Two rooms upstairs,
two rooms downstairs. There was a musty smell,
as if it had not been aired for years.

"Look at the dust," complained Aunt Janet,
pushing one of the windows open. "It'll take me
days to put the place straight."

"Well, don't start now," pleaded Grandpa,
sinking into an old armchair by the window.
"What we all need is a cup of tea and something

to eat. Open the hamper, Macpherson, my old shipmate, and take your pick. What do you fancy?"

"Kippers," said Macpherson, taking a package out of the food-hamper and licking his lips at the thought of eating them.

The hamper had been a parting gift from Miss Peacock at the shop where he worked as message-boy. It was packed to the brim with good things to eat. Eggs, butter, bacon, gingerbread, chocolate biscuits, tins of pears and peaches, and some thick black tobacco for Grandpa.

Mr McGlashan, the grocer, would never have dreamt of giving such a generous gift. Never! Not with a nickname like Old Skinflint. He had never in his life given away as much as a cracked egg or a damaged apple. But Old Skinflint was miles away in Glasgow, not at the seaside. Macpherson could easily forget him on his holidays.

"Hooray for Miss Peacock!" he cheered as the kippers began to sizzle in the frying-pan. Macpherson had good reason to cheer her, for Miss Peacock was the one who had made their dreams of a seaside holiday come true. An old cousin of hers had died, leaving Sea View and all its contents to her in his will.

"It's a pity to leave it standing empty," she said to Macpherson one day when they were both working in the back shop. Miss Peacock was the grocer's chief assistant. His right hand. But her outlook on life was very different from his. Macpherson was always pleased when he had a chance of helping her. The pair of them got on like a house on fire.

They were emptying a crate of tinned fruit, while Old Skinflint in the front shop counted the contents of the till. They could hear him mumbling to himself as he added up the money, gloating over every coin like a miser. The higher the sum went, the more satisfied his voice sounded. It was the only time of the day when the grocer seemed pleased with life.

"I have an idea," said Miss Peacock with a sparkle in her eye. "How would you like a holiday by the seaside, Macpherson?"

"Me?" Macpherson let a tin of fruit-salad slip through his fingers. "You're joking, Miss Peacock. Old Skinflint would never let me off."

But he did.

In spite of her name, Miss Peacock looked more like a plump little partridge. So meek and mild it seemed as if butter would not melt in her mouth. But when she was in a determined mood, she could always find ways and means of working miracles.

She marched resolutely into the front shop and waited till the grocer had locked up his money in the safe. Then she said, "Mr McGlashan, you remember my cousin?"

"Which one?" The grocer turned to look at her, twitching his bushy eyebrows. "You've got dozens."

"One less now," said Miss Peacock mildly. "Cousin Hector. He's dead."

Old Skinflint shot her a sharp look. "Did he leave you any money?" he asked with sudden interest.

Miss Peacock shook her head. "No, but he left me a small house at the seaside."

"You could always make money by letting it," said the grocer, with a greedy gleam in his eye.

"I'm not thinking of letting it," said Miss Peacock, getting nearer to the point.

Old Skinflint took a startled look at her. "You're not thinking of retiring?" he asked in alarm. Miss Peacock had been with him for years and years. She knew his ways. Where could he find another assistant who would work as hard, and for such low wages?

"It depends," she said craftily.

"On what?" asked the grocer, with growing alarm.

"On Macpherson. He needs a holiday. . . ."

In two minutes Mr McGlashan had given in. After all, it would be better to do without Macpherson for a fortnight than to lose Miss Peacock for ever.

"But, remember, he'll have to work all the harder when he comes back. *I* can't afford to take holidays," grumbled the grocer.

"Why not?" asked Miss Peacock boldly. "You could easily shut the shop for a while."

"Shut the shop!" The very thought made Old Skinflint shudder. Think of all the money he would lose. He glared at Miss Peacock as if she was out of her mind. "Have you finished emptying that crate?" he asked sternly.

"Not yet, Mr McGlashan. Macpherson's helping me. I'll go and see how he's getting on," said Miss Peacock, and went into the back-shop flushed with triumph. She smiled brightly at the boy and said, "I've done it! It's all settled."

Macpherson tossed a tin of pears into the air and caught it neatly as it came down. "You're a gem, Miss Peacock," he cried, catching her round the waist and dancing her up and down the shop. "A perfect gem!"

There was no doubt about it, Miss Peacock was like a fairy godmother. Macpherson would not have been surprised if she had waved a magic wand and turned Old Skinflint into a tadpole. Instead, she took a key from her pocket and said, "That's for you, Macpherson. The key to Sea View. It's all yours for a fortnight."

Sea View!

"I've seen it, Grandpa," cried Macpherson.

"Seen what, my old shipmate?"

"The sea!" Macpherson came hurtling down the stairs, two at a time. "You can see it from my bedroom window if you stand on a chair. So the name's right, after all. Sea View."

"That's great!" beamed the old man. "What else did you see, my hearty?"

"I saw the beach, and the donkeys on the sand, and the boats, and the bathers. Oh! and a lighthouse. Do you think I could go there one day, Grandpa? To the lighthouse?" asked Macpherson, eager for a new adventure.

"Why not, my boy? Nothing's impossible," said Grandpa, wagging his beard.

That was one of the best things about Grandpa. He never saw any difficulties, or spoiled any of Macpherson's ideas. It was Aunt Janet who did that.

"Don't be silly," she said crossly. "Why should anyone in their senses want to go and visit a lighthouse? Sit down and take your tea."

Grandpa winked at the boy and began to eat his kipper. "Cooked to a turn, Janet," he said, smacking his lips. Grandpa knew that a little praise sometimes worked wonders. "Nobody can fry kippers like you." He leant across to Macpherson and said, "You'll be going to explore, Captain, when you've finished your tea. You can tell me all about the lighthouse and everything when you get back."

"Are you not coming, too, Grandpa?" asked Macpherson in a disappointed voice. Everything was twice as much fun when he could share his adventures with the old man.

Grandpa shook his head. "I'll rest my old pins

for a while. I'll be quite content sitting in the garden looking at the flowers," he said cheerfully.

"And the weeds!" Aunt Janet reminded him in a grim voice.

"I'll put up with the weeds," said Grandpa, passing her his cup. "More tea, please, Janet. The sea air has sharpened my appetite already."

Macpherson left him sitting on an old wooden bench in the garden, and ran off feeling as free as air. He had no heavy message-basket to carry, no groceries to deliver, nothing to do but enjoy himself. His sandshoes felt light on his feet, and though his shorts were shabby, he was wearing a new blue-and-white striped jersey which Miss Peacock had knitted for him. It was great to be free!

He looked up at the sky and saw a seagull gliding overhead like a small aeroplane. "If I had wings I'd fly straight to the lighthouse," thought Macpherson. As it was, he used his feet and ran down the road in the direction of the sea.

It was no distance for Macpherson, who was used to walking miles in Glasgow every day. But what about Grandpa? The old man's legs were shaky. "My old pins," he called them. It would be a pity if he had to spend his holiday at Sea View and never see the sea.

"I wonder what I could do about it?" puzzled

Macpherson. In front of him he could see the sparkling water, the donkeys trotting along the sand, the people strolling on the promenade, and away out beyond the harbour the most wonderful sight of all. The lighthouse. But it would be no fun if Grandpa could not see it.

He was standing in the middle of the road, considering the problem, when he heard a shout from behind him.

"Hi, young fellow-me-lad! Get out of my way."

Macpherson whirled round and found himself face to face with a piebald pony wearing a straw hat on his head. The pony was pulling a cart driven by a strange little man, as tattered as a scarecrow. The cart was filled with junk, all jumbled together. Pots, pans, pails, fire-irons, pokers, broken chairs, cracked vases, and brass ornaments. SAM THRUMS, SCRAP-MERCHANT was painted on the side of the cart.

Sam Thrums looked as if he had been thrown on the scrap-heap himself. It seemed as if he had been patched up and put together, with some of the pieces still missing. His clothes were in rags, his face looked battered, and on his head he wore a bowler hat with a hole in the crown. But his voice was bright and cheerful.

"What's up, young fellow-me-lad? Are you day-dreaming?"

"Sorry!" said Macpherson, moving to the side to let the cart pass.

"Nothing to be sorry about," said Sam Thrums, giving him a grin. "Not on a nice day like this. Are you on holiday?"

"Yes," said Macpherson, patting the piebald pony, who was snuggling against him. "I'm staying at Sea View with Grandpa and Aunt Janet."

"Sea View!" said the man, pushing his bowler to the back of his head. "There's plenty of junk in that house! Any of it for sale?"

"I don't know," said Macpherson. "We're just visitors. It belongs to Miss Peacock. Her cousin left it to her."

"Old Hector!" said Sam Thrums, with a gleam in his eye. "A hoarder, if ever there was one. I must call in sometime and have a look round. Well, have a happy holiday, young fellow-me-lad. If there's anything I can do for you, Sam Thrum's the name. Gee-up, Soapsuds!"

As the cart began to rumble away, Macpherson had a sudden idea. "Wait, Mr Thrums," he called out. "There *is* something you can do for me. It's about Grandpa. Maybe you can help."

There and then he told the scrap-merchant all about Grandpa and his shaky pins. How was the old man ever going to see the sea if he could not walk as far as the promenade? Could anything be done to solve the problem?

Sam Thrums stopped his cart and listened intently. So did the piebald pony, who blinked his eyes and nodded his head as if he understood every word.

"It's a problem all right," said Sam Thrums, scratching his bald head as if stirring up his brains. "Let me think." Both he and the pony thought for a moment. "Perhaps I could give the old gent a lift in my cart? No! that would rattle his bones too much." He scratched his head again and then cried out, "I've got it! Yes! that's the thing!"

"What?" asked Macpherson eagerly.

"Wait and see!" said Sam Thrums, giving him a wink. "Sea View, did you say? Right! I'll see to it. Cheerio, young fellow-me-lad."

And off rattled the cart with every pot, pan and poker playing a noisy tune. Macpherson watched it go jingling round a corner, then went on his way with a lighter heart. He had a feeling that Sam Thrums, like Miss Peacock, knew how to work miracles.

"I wonder what it can be?" he thought as he ran helter-skelter down to the sea-shore.

He was soon to find out!

The Donkey-Boy

"So that's it!" gasped Macpherson when he got back to Sea View after his first visit to the beach. "It's great! Just the thing for Grandpa."

It was standing outside the door, a battered old chair, set on wheels. It was rusted and dented as if it had been through many a battle. Yet, when Macpherson gave it a push he found that the wheels ran smoothly, and the chair seemed secure enough to sit in.

"A wheel-chair. What a good idea!" he cried, sitting in it himself to try it out. "It'll solve Grandpa's problems."

No need to wonder who had brought it. Soapsuds, the piebald pony, was tethered to the crumbling gatepost. Now and again he stretched his neck over the fence to nibble at a nettle. Then he nodded his head in its straw hat and grinned at Macpherson as if saying, "What do you think of that, young fellow-me-lad? Sam Thrums always keeps his word."

When Macpherson opened the door he could hear the junk-man's cheerful voice. Sam Thrums was sitting at the table, drinking tea and eating a slice of Miss Peacock's gingerbread. He and Grandpa seemed to be on friendly terms already, but Aunt Janet was looking down her nose at him in a cold manner.

"I'm warning you," she was saying to Grandpa. "It'll fall to pieces, and then where will you be? It's not safe."

"Safe as houses," said Sam Thrums, stirring another spoonful of sugar into his tea. "It only needs a few screws and a bit of spit-and-polish." He looked at Macpherson. "What's your opinion, young fellow-me-lad?"

"Super!" said Macpherson. "It looks smashing."

"Smashed, if you ask me," said Aunt Janet in a grim voice.

"Nonsense, Janet woman," said Grandpa, peering out of the window to take another look at the chair. "It'll soon be ship-shape. I can hardly wait to set sail." He turned to Macpherson. "It was lucky you met Mr Thrums. He has been very kind."

"Huh!" sniffed Aunt Janet. "You haven't asked him how much it will cost."

"Nothing," said Sam Thrums, beaming at her in his friendly way. "You've paid for it already, lassie, with this cup of tea. The best I've ever tasted."

He raised his battered bowler to Aunt Janet, who went red in the face. She was not used, at her time of life, to being called a lassie. For once she had nothing sharp to say.

"Thanks, Mr Thrums," said Grandpa gratefully. "D'you know what, Macpherson? Mr Thrums has been telling me that he goes out in the lifeboat."

"Goodness gracious!" cried Macpherson, looking at the man with new interest. "When?"

"I can be called out at any time of the day or night," Sam Thrums told him. "When I hear the rocket going off, that's the signal. Soapsuds knows the sound, too. Believe it or not, he turns right round in his tracks and trots straight to the lifeboat-station."

"Mercy!" said Macpherson, wide-eyed with wonder. He stared enviously at the junk-man. "I hope the rocket goes off while I'm here. It must be great to be a member of a lifeboat-crew."

But there was better to follow.

"You should meet my brother Davy," said Sam Thrums, accepting a fill of Grandpa's tobacco for his pipe. It was an old-fashioned one, with a second-hand look about it, like everything of Sam's. "Davy's the one for the sea. Hates living ashore, does Davy."

"Oh! where does he live, then?" wondered Macpherson.

"In the lighthouse," said Sam Thrums, pointing his pipe in the direction of the sea.

Macpherson gave a loud "Whoop" of delight and began to sizzle with excitement, like a kettle about to boil over. "Did you hear that, Grandpa? The lighthouse! Oh, Mr Thrums, do you think your brother Davy would let me. . . ?"

"Why not?" Sam Thrums grinned at Macpherson. "Leave it to me, young fellow-me-lad. I'll see to it."

Macpherson gripped the man's hand and pumped it up and down. "What luck!" he cried, almost beside himself with joy. "Oh my! I *am* glad I met you."

"I'm well worth meeting!" beamed the junk-man, rising to his feet. He took a keen look round the kitchen, at the rocking-chair, the china dogs on the mantelpiece, and the old crockery on the dresser. "Anything for sale?" he asked with a gleam in his eye.

"It depends on Miss Peacock," Grandpa told him. "Maybe she'll want to get rid of some of it. It's her house. She'll be coming down to visit us on Saturday, I hope."

"Right! Tell her Sam Thrums's ready to do a deal with her," he said, making for the door. "You'll remember the name?"

"I'm not likely to forget it," said Grandpa

warmly. "Drop in any time you like, Mr Thrums. You'll always be welcome. Isn't that so, Janet?"

"M-m!" said Aunt Janet, which was as near to a warm invitation as Sam Thrums was likely to get from her.

Macpherson went out and helped him to patch up the wheel-chair. He was longing to talk about the lighthouse, but Sam kept him busy tightening screws, polishing handles and straightening out spokes of the wheels.

Finally he dusted the seat and said proudly, "There! it's fit for a king. Fetch the old gent and take him for a spin."

Macpherson ran into the house, calling eagerly, "We're ready to set sail. Come aboard, Grandpa."

The old man shuffled out on his shaky pins and seated himself in the chair, with Aunt Janet fussing after him with a rug to tuck round his knees.

"You be careful," she warned Macpherson. "Don't push too hard or it'll run away from you. I don't trust that chair, nor you either."

"Fiddlesticks! It's as safe as houses, and so is the young fellow-me-lad," said Sam Thrums, giving her a reassuring pat on the shoulder. "Why not come, too, lassie? You're welcome to ride in my cart."

The "lassie" took a look at the higgledy-piggledy cart and at the piebald pony with his straw hat to the one side. "Amongst all that junk? Never!" she said, turning her back on Sam.

"Wait and see!" he said, digging Macpherson in the ribs. "Your auntie'll be driving the pony before the week's out. Are you all set?"

"Anchors away!" said Grandpa, settling back in the chair.

"Ay, ay, sir," cried Macpherson, giving the chair a push up the garden path. Soapsuds blew down his nose at them in a friendly fashion, and Sam Thrums waved his bowler. They were off.

The chair trundled smoothly down the road leading to the shore.

"Like sailing the seas," chuckled Grandpa, gazing ahead at the sparkling water. "Ahoy, Macpherson, I can see your lighthouse. Isn't it a fine sight? Bless my old bones! it's great to be at the seaside without having to walk a single step."

Macpherson pushed the creaking chair along the promenade, while Grandpa sat back and sniffed in the sea-breezes. His old eyes were sharp enough to notice everything. The donkeys trotting along the sand, the boats bobbing up and down in the water, the bathers splashing in the sea, and the gulls circling around in the air.

Suddenly he sat up and said, "Shiver me timbers! Macpherson, do you see what I see?"

"Where, Grandpa?"

"There! Straight ahead."

A small figure was trudging towards them, pushing an old pram, every bit as battered as the wheel-chair. She wore a dress many sizes too big for her, hitched up at the side with a safety-pin. Her face was almost hidden by a large floppy hat. But there was no mistaking who she was.

"Maisie Murphy!" gasped Macpherson, stopping suddenly in his tracks.

"Yeth, it'th me, Macpherthon," she lisped, hurrying towards them. "Ith thith not a thurprithe?"

"Surprise!' said Macpherson, staring at the small, chubby girl. "I'm bamboozled!"

No wonder! The last time he had seen little Miss Murphy she had been at home in Glasgow. He was not sure whether he was glad or sorry to see her now. At home he saw enough of her every day, for Maisie lived in the same skyscraper and followed him around like a faithful puppy. Trying to shake off Maisie was one of his daily deeds. And now here she was, as large as life, at the seaside.

All the same, Macpherson had a soft spot for her. Poor Maisie led a hard life. She had to act as nursemaid to the large brood of Murphy children. Today she was in charge of the latest baby, lying asleep in the shabby old pram.

"I'm on holiday," she told him brightly. "I've been taking Thinderella for a wee walk."

"Cinderella," said Macpherson, peering at the sleeping child. "Is that her?"

"Yeth. We haven't got a name for her yet, tho I'm calling her Thinderella in the meantime," said Maisie, giving the pram a little shoogle backwards and forwards.

"Well, you're certainly not an Ugly Sister, my dear," said Grandpa, looking at Maisie's rosy cheeks and bright eyes. "That's a splendid hat you're wearing."

"Ithn't it?" said Maisie proudly. "It came from

a Jumble Thale." She stared at Grandpa's chair. "Oh, that'th a funny pram."

"It's not a pram, silly. It's a wheel-chair," said Macpherson, putting her in her place. When Maisie was around he always felt superior. Yet, in the end, it was sometimes Maisie who taught him a lesson.

"Fanthy!" Maisie had never seen such a thing before, not even at a Jumble Sale. "It'th great!"

Everything was great to Maisie. She was on her holidays, she was wearing her best hat, she had met her hero, Macpherson. What more could she want? Nothing! There was a look of bliss on her round, cheerful face.

"Where are you staying, Maisie, my dear?" Grandpa asked her.

"There!" said Maisie, pointing vaguely in the direction of Sea View. "With Mr Thrumth."

"Not Tham Thrumth? I mean Sam Thrums," cried Macpherson. It was difficult not to lisp when talking to Maisie.

"Yeth," said she, nodding her head in its floppy hat. "He thleepth in the thtable."

"Sleeps in the stable!" cried Macpherson, not believing her.

The floppy hat nodded once more. "The pony thleepth there, too. And a donkey called Thilly-Willy."

"You're a silly-willy yourself," scoffed Macpherson. He was never too sure whether Maisie was telling the truth or making up tarradiddles.

"There he ith!" She waved wildly to someone on the sand. "Thilly-Willy! Yoo-hoo!"

A fat donkey, ambling along the seashore, turned and gave a loud "Ee-haw!" as if calling "Yoo-hoo!" back to her. A barefoot boy at his side waved a greeting to Maisie.

"That'th Mungo," she explained. "He thleepth in the thtable, too."

"Shiver my timbers!" cried Grandpa. "How many more?"

"Only the cockth and henth."

Maisie looked wistfully at the donkey, then at the baby sleeping in the pram. She gave a little sigh and said, "Mungo'th going to let me have a ride on Thilly-Willy one day." But Maisie knew that, even though she was on holiday, duty must come first.

Grandpa twinkled his eyes at her and said, "Off you go, my dear, and enjoy yourself. You, too, Macpherson. I'll sit here for a while and stare at the sea. If Cinderella wakes up, I'll sing her a sea-shanty. *Yo-ho-ho! and a bottle of rum!*"

Maisie flung her arms round the old man's neck and cried, "Oh, thankth, Grandpa." She gave him a smacking kiss on his wrinkled cheek, and

then said to Macpherson, "Come on; let'th go."
Not one moment of her freedom must be wasted.

Macpherson hesitated. "Are you sure you'll be
all right, Grandpa?" he asked anxiously.

"Certain sure." The old man turned his chair
round so that he could have a better view of the
sea. "Don't worry, my old shipmate. Cinderella
and I can look after each other."

Maisie clutched Macpherson by the hand and
danced along the promenade, as gay as a lark.

"Ithn't it *lovely*?" she cried, as they ran down
the steps leading to the shore. Maisie lived for the
moment and could be happier than a queen with
very little. A lollipop to suck, some cast-off finery
to wear, or, best of all, Macpherson by her side.

It was wonderful to feel the soft sand under their
feet and the sea-breezes whipping the colour into
their cheeks. They took off their sandshoes, raced
along the beach and waded into the water.

Maisie hitched up her trailing skirts and scream-
ed with pleasure as the frothy waves came swirling
round her bare legs. Her cheeks were rosy-red,
and she had forgotten all about Cinderella and
her never-ending duties as nursemaid.

Suddenly she gazed out beyond the harbour
and said, "Oh look, Macpherthon! What'th that?"

"That?" Macpherson looked at the lighthouse
standing sturdily in the sea with the waves break-

ing around its base. "That's a lighthouse, of course."

His heart began to beat faster when he thought he would soon be sailing out to explore it. He would have liked to boast about it to Maisie. But she would only want to come, too. It was best to keep it a secret.

She was staring up at him in admiration. "You know everything, Macpherthon," she said, breathing heavily. "You're tho clever."

"That's right! I'm a genius!" scoffed Macpherson. "Come on, you silly wee dumpling. I want to meet Mungo and the donkey."

All the donkeys were standing in a little group near the pier, waiting for customers. All except Silly-Willy. Although he was the fattest and slowest he seemed to be the most popular. Everyone wanted to ride on the shaggy little creature, and Mungo was kept busy lifting small children on to the donkey's back and taking them for trots along the sand.

They shrieked with delight at Silly-Willy's capers. Sometimes he went sideways; sometimes he went round in circles as if dancing a waltz; sometimes he came to a sudden standstill and refused to move. Or he would rock back and forwards like a rocking-horse. There was no knowing what the funny little donkey would do next.

The other donkey-boys hated Silly-Willy because of his popularity. Hated Mungo, too, as so many people wanted to ride his donkey. But Mungo himself seemed bright and cheerful.

He was small and freckle-faced, with a bush of red, curly hair. He seemed strong and sturdy enough, yet he was so under-sized that he found it difficult to reach up and steady his young customers to keep them from falling off. Especially when Silly-Willy was in a frisky mood.

"Poor Mungo," said Maisie, watching the boy's

attempts to keep up with Silly-Willy. "He hath no mother or father. Tho Mr Thrumth lookth after him. Oh dear! he'th tumbled down."

The donkey-boy had stumbled and was lying sprawled on the sand. Before he could get up, Silly-Willy had taken to his heels, with a small golden-haired child clinging to his back. She began to look frightened when she realized she was on her own.

"I'll fall off!" she wailed, bursting into tears.

One of the other donkey-boys, a big, rough-looking lad, picked up a handful of pebbles from the beach. "Let her fall off!" he shouted. "It'll serve Mungo right. He takes all the customers away from us."

With that, he gave a loud yell and let fly with the pebbles. They flew straight to their target and hit the donkey on his hind leg.

"Ee-haw! Ee-haw!" brayed Silly-Willy, tossing his head in alarm.

Then, to everyone's horror, he swerved straight into the sea.

With a wild scream of terror the little girl fell off and vanished beneath the waves.

3

Strange Adventures

"Mac-pher-thon!" wailed Maisie Murphy, prancing from one foot to another at the edge of the sea. "Come back! You'll get drownded!"

Macpherson did not hear her. Not that he would have taken any notice if he had. Without waiting to think, he had waded waist-deep into the water and plunged beneath the waves.

Silly-Willy was standing in the sea, looking about him in a daze, as if wondering what had happened. But where was the little girl who had fallen off his back? There was no sign of her.

Macpherson did the breast-stroke and the crawl as best he could. He had only started taking swimming lessons at the public baths in Glasgow, and this was the first time he had tried to swim in the sea. In the baths he had never been away from the shallow end. Now he was out of his depth.

"Mac-pher-thon!"

Maisie gave another shriek of alarm when his head vanished under the water. Then she saw his hand reach out, grab a floating figure and try to hold her up. Just in time another helping hand came to his aid. Mungo had struggled to his feet and rushed into the sea. In spite of his small size, the donkey-boy was a strong swimmer.

"Leave her to me!" he called to Macpherson. He grabbed the child and held her up. Then he turned on his back and floated to the shore, dragging her with him.

Macpherson gulped a great mouthful of sea-water and shook himself like a terrier. He felt a little ashamed of himself when he saw how much better Mungo could swim. He resolved to go to the baths more often when he got home.

Maisie, too, was in the water by now, with her long skirt floating around her. She tripped and sat down with a bump beside the donkey, crying, "Oh, Macpherthon, are you drownded?"

"No, I'm not, silly!" said Macpherson, hauling her up. "Come and help the wee girl."

Mungo was kneeling on the sand beside the girl, trying to revive her. Already the colour was coming back to her cheeks, and soon she began to cough and splutter. Then she started to sob with fright.

"It's all right," said Mungo soothingly. "You're safe now."

"I'm s-s-soaking wet," she wailed, pushing her

drenched hair back from her face. "I want my Nanny."

Maisie went and sat beside her. She was used to dealing with young children, especially when they were having tantrums. "Thtop it!" she said firmly. "There'th nothing to cry about. You'll thoon get dry."

The little girl sat up and stared at Maisie through her tears.

"Who are you?" she asked, rubbing her eyes.

"I'm Maithie Murphy and I'm wet, too. But *I*'m not crying. Come on; let'th run along the thand to get dry."

She took hold of the child's hand and was pulling her up when a stout woman came hurrying along the shore. She was out of breath and her face was flushed with anger.

"Leave that child alone!" she shouted to Maisie. "What have you been doing to her?" She stared in alarm at the little girl. "Oh! my poor darling. You're soaked to the skin."

She knelt down on the sand and put her arms round the child, who burst into another flood of tears. "Oh, Nanny, I fell off the donkey into the s-s-sea. . . ."

"My poor pet," said the stout woman, taking a towel from her bag and beginning to rub the child dry. "Nanny's here. You're quite safe now.

We must hurry back to the hotel and change your wet clothes. But first I want a word with that donkey-boy."

Her face grew redder as she turned and glared at Mungo. "Did I not tell you to keep an eye on her while I went to buy a newspaper?" she raged, shaking her fist at him. "Two minutes only! And look what happened as soon as my back was turned."

"I'm sorry," began Mungo; but the woman would not listen. She was working herself up into a great passion.

"Sorry! You'll be sorrier! I've a good mind to

fetch a policeman. You might have killed her little Ladyship."

The woman was in such a rage by now that even Silly-Willy shrank back and turned tail. But Maisie Murphy was fearless. She faced up to her and said fiercely, "Don't be thilly. Mungo thaved the wee girl, and tho did Macpherthon. Anyway, it wath your own fault for not being with her. Tho there!"

The woman grew even more scarlet, through guilt as well as anger.

"How dare you talk to me like that?" she shouted. "You're a rude ignorant lot." She caught the child by the hand and said, "Come with me, Lady Sarah, away from those nasty rough creatures."

But the little girl had recovered herself by now and was looking at Maisie and the others with great interest. "Oh Nanny, can't I stay?" she pleaded. "I'd like to play with them. And I want another ride on the donkey."

"No, you can't," said the woman crossly. "Come along with Nanny at once." And she dragged away the little girl, who kept looking round and waving back to the group she had left behind.

"What'th a Nanny?" asked Maisie in a puzzled voice.

"She's a kind of nurse," explained Mungo, who

40

was rubbing Silly-Willy dry. "They're staying at the Beach Hotel. The little girl's a Lady, and her grandmother's a Duchess."

"Merthy me!" Maisie was amazed to think that such a small child could be a real Lady. She was thoughtful for a moment, and then she said, "Maybe I'll be a Nanny when I grow up." She knew there was no hope of her being a Lady.

"You!" scoffed Macpherson. "You're a nanny already. Come on; we'd better all run about and get dry. Then we'll have to go back to Grandpa and Cinderella."

They ran races along the sand, jumped on and off the little donkey's back, and laughed merrily when Silly-Willy waltzed round in circles. The other donkey-boys watched them from a distance, looking a trifle ashamed of themselves. Especially when Maisie went up to the rough lad who had caused all the trouble.

"I think you're a big bully," she said, stamping her small foot at him. "I hope you're thorry. Go on! Thay you're thorry."

The donkey-boy looked down at her and turned scarlet round the ears. Then he mumbled something that sounded like "Sorry!", after which Maisie beamed on him brightly and said, "That'th better." Little Miss Murphy could never be angry with anyone for long.

"Come along," said Macpherson, taking her firmly by the hand. "We must get back to Grandpa." He took a last look at the lighthouse and turned to Mungo. "Have you ever been there?"

"Yes, heaps of times. My Uncle Sam takes me."

"Lucky thing!" said Macpherson enviously. But perhaps he, too, was going to be lucky, if Mr Thrums kept his word. And he had a feeling that the junk-man never let anyone down.

Their clothes were almost dry by now, and Maisie and Macpherson looked none the worse of their wetting by the time they ran back to join Grandpa.

"Saw it all!" said the old man, sitting up in his wheel-chair. "And so did Cinderella. Blow me down! what adventures you have, Macpherson, my old shipmate." He winked at the boy and said, "Better not tell Aunt Janet. You know what she would say!"

Macpherson nodded his head, and began to push Grandpa home in the chair while Maisie wheeled the pram at his side. When they reached Sea View the old man took a deep breath and said, "I feel years younger already. Years! I hope Janet has the kettle boiling. I could do with a cup of tea and a bite to eat. What about you, Maisie?"

No need to ask. "I'm thtarving," said Maisie.

Even without the sea-air Maisie was always ready for food.

"Maisie Murphy," said Aunt Janet sternly, "it's high time you took that baby away home."

That baby was lying on the rug, kicking her bare feet and making goo-goo noises at Grandpa. Aunt Janet could not bring herself to call the child by such a foolish name as Cinderella. Unlike Maisie, she had no time for fairy-tales.

"I'll go thoon," said Maisie, but she made no move to leave the table. Not till she had finished off the last bite of gingerbread.

They had all been fed. Even the baby, who had taken little sips of warm milk and was licking her lips as if asking for more. All the Murphy clan had hearty appetites, but none better than Maisie. She had sampled everything Aunt Janet had set on the table. The last of the chocolate biscuits had gone, and the food-hamper was almost empty.

"I'll have to go down to the shops tomorrow," sighed Aunt Janet, clearing away the empty dishes. "It'll be a long trail, carrying the groceries back."

"Cheer up, Janet woman. I'll lend you my wheel-chair," offered Grandpa. He grinned at Macpherson behind her back. "Or maybe you would rather have a lift in Mr Thrums's cart?"

Aunt Janet tossed her head. "I'd sooner crawl on my hands and knees." She stood over Maisie and said crossly. "Did you hear me, Maisie Murphy? Take that baby away home."

"Yeth. Okay." Maisie went and lifted the baby from the rug. "Come on, Thinderella. I'll put you back in the pram."

The pram was parked at the door side-by-side with the wheel-chair. To Maisie's delight, Macpherson came with her, helping to push the pram up the bumpy road towards the holiday-house which the Murphys had rented from Sam Thrums.

It was a tumbledown house with an untidy clutter of rubbish lying about in the garden. A swarm of children were playing happily with a broken bicycle, and Murphy himself was sitting on the doorstep in his shirt-sleeves, sunning himself and smoking his pipe.

"Hullo, me boyo," he called out to Macpherson. "How are you enjoying your holidays?"

"Fine. And you, Mr Murphy?"

"Tip-top!" said Murphy, leaning back and stretching himself.

"Keep an eye on Thinderella," Maisie said firmly to her father, parking the pram beside him. "Macpherthon'th coming with me to thee the thtable. Thith way."

She led Macpherson round the corner to another

broken-down building. Inside there was a clutter of second-hand goods. Old bedsteads, broken chairs, pots, pans, kettles, and cracked jugs, all heaped together. A few cocks and hens pecked on the ground, and Sam Thrums was there feeding the piebald pony.

"Come in, young fellow-me-lad," he cried, turning round to welcome Macpherson. "I see you've met up with Miss Murphy."

"Yes, and I've met up with Mungo and Silly-Willy, too," said Macpherson, gazing around the untidy stable. "Where do you sleep, Mr Thrums?"

"Come and I'll show you," said the junk-man. He stepped over a hen and led Macpherson to a dim corner of the stable. Two hammocks were hung from the rafters, with a heap of hay underneath. "The donkey sleeps in the hay," explained Sam Thrums, "and Mungo and I sleep in the hammocks, nice and snug."

"Fancy that!" said Macpherson, intrigued with this unusual bedroom. "May I try, Mr Thrums?"

"Go ahead, young fellow-me-lad."

Macpherson hoisted himself up into one of the hammocks and lay there, swaying backwards and forwards till he almost lulled himself to sleep. It must be fun, he thought, to float off into dreamland in this cosy stable, with the animals for company.

Then he remembered his own little bedroom at Sea View. Perhaps tonight he would see the lighthouse flashing out its friendly beams across the water. He would go to sleep and dream of the day when he would sail out to visit it.

"Oh, lucky me!" he thought, as he swung to and fro. "The start of the holidays, and ever so many adventures to come!"

It was not long before the adventures began. Next day a strange thing happened.

Macpherson and Grandpa were away out beyond the harbour in a small boat, rowing with one oar each. An oary-boat, the old man called it. Very different from the great ships in which he had once sailed the seas. Yet Grandpa looked as pleased as if he was in command of a great ocean liner.

"Heave-ho, my hearty!" he cried, dipping his oar in the water. "Steady does it. In-out. In-out."

Macpherson wiped the sweat from his brow with one hand and looked admiringly at Grandpa. It was great being out in an oary-boat with such a splendid old sea-dog. Grandpa seemed as strong as a giant. No need to worry about his shaky pins now that he was back where he belonged. On the sea. If they kept going at this rate, they might even get as far as the lighthouse.

The trouble was the lighthouse seemed to be farther and farther away, no matter how quickly they rowed. Outside the harbour the open sea was choppier. The boat creaked as it mounted the waves, and Macpherson had to tug hard on his oar with both hands. But Grandpa did not seem to feel the strain. He had the right knack.

"Ho-ro! keep it up, my hearty," said he, beaming at the boy. "This is the life!"

No doubt about it, the holiday was doing Grandpa a world of good. Already there was more colour in his cheeks and a sparkle in his eye. When Macpherson had pushed him down to the shore in his wheel-chair, the old man had insisted in getting out and taking a short stroll along the sand. But walking beside the sea was not enough. Grandpa felt the old urge to sail on it.

Macpherson was walking by his side when Grandpa pointed to a notice. BOATS FOR HIRE.

"Are you game, Macpherson?" he asked eagerly.

"Yes, Grandpa. I'm game for anything."

They went off without telling Aunt Janet, like two schoolboys playing truant. She was sitting bolt upright on the sand, staring at the sea as if she did not approve of it. Certainly she would not have approved of Grandpa launching an oary-boat into the water. Luckily, she did not notice until it was too late.

The *Seagull* was bobbing over the waves well out of her reach before she realized who was on board. Macpherson saw her spring to her feet and hurry to the water's edge, calling out to them in angry tones. But they pretended not to hear. She could be as cross as she liked as long as they were safely out of her way.

They were out of Maisie's way, too. Little Miss Murphy was at home looking after Cinderella who had suddenly broken out in spots. Measles? Or only an upset tummy? No one could tell till the doctor came. Meantime, Maisie was tied to her task as nursemaid. It was hard lines on her, yet Macpherson was glad to be left alone with Grandpa.

"Could we row as far as the lighthouse, Grandpa?" asked Macpherson, tugging at his oar. His arms were aching, but as long as the old man kept going, he was would not give in.

"Not in this old tub, Macpherson my boy," said Grandpa, peering ahead at the rough sea. "Right about turn! We've gone far enough for one day. Pull for the shore."

"Ay, ay, Captain!"

It was disappointing, yet Macpherson knew Grandpa was right. They turned the creaking little boat round and rowed for the shelter of the harbour. The figures on the shore seemed very small and far away, like pygmies playing on the sand. Macpherson could see the donkeys trotting along the beach, but he could not tell which was Silly-Willy or which of the boys was Mungo. Yet there was no mistaking the upright figure pacing by the water's edge. Aunt Janet was waiting to give them a warm welcome.

"Oh my! I wish I could stay out on the sea for ever and ever," sighed Macpherson. And not only because of Aunt Janet. He was beginning to understand why Grandpa loved it so much. There was something soothing about the movement of the waves. Up-down! Up-down! It would be great to sail right round the world.

Suddenly he was startled out of his reverie by Grandpa's warning cry.

"Ship ahoy! Watch out, Macpherson! Danger ahead!"

Macpherson looked up and saw a speed-boat hurtling towards them as if it meant to mow them down. The boat bounced over the waves, sending great sprays of water high into the air. Its powerful engine was roaring like a raging lion.

"Pull, Macpherson, pull!" cried Grandpa, tugging desperately at his oar in an effort to avoid a collision.

But it seemed that only a miracle could save them.

4

Macpherson's Helping Hand

Macpherson gritted his teeth and pulled at his oar with all his might. The next moment he was blinded by a shower of icy-cold water as the boat went speeding by, missing the *Seagull* by a whisker. The miracle had happened.

Macpherson hastily brushed the water from his eyes in time to catch a glimpse of a young man in a yachting-cap, grinning back at them as if pleased with his performance. Then the speed-boat raced off as if nothing had happened.

"Idiot!" shouted Grandpa; but the speed-boat had zigzagged out beyond the harbour, leaving the little *Seagull* pitching and tossing in its wake.

"I'd like to teach that young fellow a few lessons," said Grandpa grimly, wiping the salt spray from his face. But he could never be downhearted for long. "Never mind, Macpherson, my hearty," he beamed. "We're lucky to be alive."

Not so lucky when they reached the shore. Aunt Janet had been bottling up her rage, and it was Macpherson who had to bear the brunt of it.

"You're a fine one!" she stormed at him,

shaking him by the shoulders. "Have you no sense, taking an old man out in a boat like that, at his time of life? Behind my back, too. You might have been drowned. What would you have said then?"

"Nothing," said Macpherson meekly. It was no use arguing with Aunt Janet when she was in one of her tempers.

"Calm down, Janet woman," said Grandpa, coming to the rescue. "There's no harm done. We'll take you with us next time."

"Fiddlesticks!" said Aunt Janet crossly. She gave Macpherson another shaking. "As for you, you can come with me and make yourself useful. I have some shopping to do, so you can carry the groceries back home. It'll keep you out of mischief. Then there's the gate to mend, and the garden to weed, and. . . ."

"Stop, woman, stop!" cried Grandpa, putting his hands to his ears. "We're on our holidays, not on hard labour."

All the same, they went with her for the sake of peace. Grandpa got into his wheel-chair and sat outside the General Store while Macpherson went inside with Aunt Janet and waited till she had made her purchases.

It was a very different shop from Mr Mc-Glashan's in Glasgow. The customers were all chatting to each other in a friendly fashion, and a black cat lay snoozing on the counter. The grocer was a fat, cheerful man who seemed to like nothing better than giving away free samples.

"Try one of these apples," he said to a customer. "Help yourself to a biscuit," he told another. "Taste this new cheese," said he, offering a piece to Aunt Janet.

Old Skinflint would have gone mad!

"Lovely weather for the holidays," he said, beaming across the counter at Aunt Janet. "What can I get for you? Take your time and have a good look round." He handed a peppermint to Macpherson. "Here's something for you, young man."

"Oh thanks!" said Macpherson. He sucked his way round the shop while Aunt Janet made her purchases. He wished he could work in a place like this, within sight of the sea, and with never a cross word from his employer. Better than trudging round the busy streets of Glasgow. Yet, Glasgow was home, and he liked it in spite of Old Skinflint. Indeed, Macpherson – like Maisie Murphy – could be happy anywhere. He was used to making the best of everything.

Suddenly he swallowed the peppermint in one gulp. He had caught sight of a picture on the front page of the local paper, lying beside the cat on the counter. It was a picture of an old lady, with a young man and a little girl standing beside her.

"Mercy me! it's him. The young man in the speed-boat," thought Macpherson, staring at the picture. "And that's the wee girl who fell into the sea." He read the caption underneath.

"The Duchess of Oakbank is staying at the Beach Hotel, with her grandson, Lord Ronald, and her little granddaughter, Lady Sarah. . . ."

"Macpherson!"

Aunt Janet's harsh voice interrupted him. "Come and help me," she said in an irritated voice. She dumped a large parcel of groceries into his arms. "Stop day-dreaming and carry these home."

The grocer gave him a sympathetic smile and said, "So long, young man. Have a happy holiday."

Macpherson blinked his eyes when he went out into the bright sunshine. Then he opened them wide with surprise when he saw that Grandpa was not alone. Another wheel-chair was drawn up beside his, a very different kind from the old wreck in which Grandpa was sitting. This one was well-sprung, new and shiny, with soft cushions and not a dent or a scratch to be seen on it.

An old lady was sitting in it, like a queen on a

throne. Indeed, the little lace bonnet she wore on her soft, white hair looked like a crown. There was a glitter of gold round her neck, and the diamonds in her rings sparkled in the sun. Grandpa looked like a shabby old scarecrow beside her.

Macpherson gave a gasp when he saw her. It was the old lady in the newspaper picture. The Duchess of Oakbank. Grandpa was chatting to her as if he had known her all his life, and the Duchess was leaning forward to catch every word he said.

Aunt Janet said impatiently, "Who is he talking to now? Really! he's the limit! I'm going home without him."

She marched off with her head in the air, leaving Macpherson shifting his bundle of groceries from one arm to the other.

Grandpa looked up and called, "Ahoy, Macpherson, my hearty! Come and join us."

The Duchess turned to look at him. "So this is Macpherson," she said in a soft, sweet voice. "Let me have a look at you. Your grandfather has been telling me all sorts of interesting things about you."

"Oh yes, Macpherson's always up to something interesting. Wait till you hear what happened today when we were out in the *Seagull*," chuckled Grandpa, who always enjoyed having a tale to tell. "We were nearly killed by a silly young idiot...."

"Grandpa!" said Macpherson, trying to stop him. His face went red. "It's time we went home."

"Nonsense, my boy. Why worry about time when we're on holiday? Let me finish my story. This young fool...."

"Grandpa!" said Macpherson desperately.

The old man looked at him in surprise. "What's the hurry, shipmate?" he asked. "You seem very anxious to get me away."

Macpherson shuffled his feet, not knowing

what to say. How could he get Grandpa to understand?

The Duchess was smiling at him in her gentle way. Then she turned to the old man and said, "You're lucky to have someone like Macpherson to look after you. Not like my grandson. He promised to come and take me back to the hotel, but I expect he has forgotten." She sighed. "I'm afraid he's rather selfish. Too much money, and too little to do, that's Ronald's trouble."

"Well, it's not Macpherson's," said Grandpa, with a grin. "Not that we bother much about money. We have plenty of fun without it. Don't we, my old shipmate?"

"Y-Yes," agreed Macpherson; but he was not so sure. It might be better fun to be a millionaire and buy a split-new wheel-chair for Grandpa. Or even a helicopter to take him for trips round the world. Yet when he saw the old man's clear eyes and glowing cheeks, he knew Grandpa was right. The best things in life could not be bought.

Feeling more cheerful, he turned to the Duchess and said, "If you like, ma'am, I'll take you back to your hotel." He dumped the groceries in Grandpa's arms. "Wait for me, Grandpa. I won't be long. It isn't far to the Beach Hotel."

The old lady looked up at him in surprise.

"How did you know where I am staying?" she wondered.

Macpherson's face flushed. "I – I saw your picture in the newspaper," he confessed.

"Dear me! So you know who I am," she said in an amused voice.

"Yes, ma'am. The Duchess of Oakbank."

Grandpa almost let the groceries drop from his grip. "Bless my bones!" he cried out. "A Duchess! And me talking to you as if you were an ordinary human being!"

"Very ordinary, I assure you," said the Duchess, smiling at him, "and very human, too." She reached across to shake his hand. "Thank you for your lively conversation. I *have* enjoyed myself. I do hope we'll meet again."

"Shiver my timbers!" said Grandpa, blinking his eyes at her. "A real live Duchess!"

He sat clutching the groceries and staring after her while Macpherson wheeled the old lady away. It was easier than pushing Grandpa's rickety chair. Everything ran so smoothly, and his passenger seemed as light as a feather.

They were nearing the hotel when the Duchess turned to him and said, "I didn't hear the end of your grandfather's story about your narrow escape on the sea. Tell me what happened, Macpherson."

"Oh, it was nothing, ma'am," said Macpherson

uneasily. "Just a young man in a speed-boat. . . ."

"I can guess!" said the old lady, sitting up. "My grandson, Ronald. Careless creature! He has been spoilt, that's what's wrong with him. He never thinks of anyone but himself."

She seemed more amused than angry. And Macpherson realized that, if the young man was selfish and spoilt, it was partly the Duchess's fault.

"It doesn't matter," he said hastily. "There was no damage done."

The Beach Hotel was like a great castle with towers and turrets, set in a garden full of bright flowers with a fountain in the middle. Some of the guests were sitting sunning themselves in deck-chairs, and sprawling on the grass was the young man who had been out in the speed-boat.

"Ronald, darling," called the Duchess as Macpherson wheeled her up the drive. "Come here, you naughty boy."

The young man rose to his feet and said carelessly, "Oh hullo, Granny, I was just coming to fetch you."

She looked at him fondly and said, "Well, you have been saved the trouble. Lazy boy! *I* know what happened. You went out sailing and forgot all about your poor old grandmother."

He shrugged his shoulders, then stretched himself lazily. "I was so bored, I had to do something." He took a casual glance at Macpherson. "Who is he?"

"Macpherson," said the Duchess, "and you owe him an apology. He and his grandfather were out in a rowing-boat, and you nearly ran them down."

"Really?" said the young man casually. "Well, they should have kept out of my way. Anyway, rowing-boats ought to be banned. They are a nuisance, and these holiday-makers are too stupid to know how to handle them."

Macpherson's face flushed with anger. "My grandpa's not stupid!" he cried; then he bit back his words. What was the use of making a scene in front of the old lady? Better to hurry away and let his anger cool down.

"Wait," said the young man, thrusting his hand in his pocket. "I expect you'll want to be paid for your services. How much?"

Macpherson gave him a straight cool look. "Nothing, thank you," he said evenly. Then he turned to the Duchess. "Goodbye, ma'am," and ran quickly away down the drive. If that was what being rich did to people, he was glad he and Grandpa were poor. There were better things to think about. The lighthouse, for example. And goodness knew how many more adventures to come.

The very next day it happened. A new adventure!

"Gee-up, Soapsuds!" cried Macpherson, sitting beside Maisie Murphy in Sam Thrums's rickety junk-cart. The piebald pony looked round at him and grinned. But he did not gee-up. He just plodded on at his usual slow and steady pace. Soapsuds was not the one to hurry if he could help it.

They were jogging along a quiet country road, still within sight of the sea. The cart was empty except for Macpherson and Maisie. Sam Thrums was walking behind it, keeping a look-out for any cottage where he might pick up some old scrap.

"Thith ith great!" cried Maisie, beaming with joy. "I'm ever tho happy." She was in her element, handling the reins like a cow-girl and wearing the pony's straw hat on her tousled head.

Cinderella was asleep in her pram at Sea View. ("Just a tummy upset; she'll soon be all right," the doctor had said). Grandpa had promised to keep an eye on her while he mended the garden gate, and Maisie and Macpherson were free to enjoy themselves.

Aunt Janet had scolded the old man for his sudden burst of energy. "You'll suffer for it," she warned him. "Why can't you sit still and let Macpherson do the work?"

"Because I want to do it myself," said Grandpa stubbornly. "Stop ordering me about, Janet woman. I like the feel of a hammer in my hand." He beamed at Macpherson. "Off you go, my old shipmate, and be sure to tell me all about it when you come back."

Like Maisie, Macpherson felt as happy as a lark, rattling along the road in the creaking cart. Sunshine and sea-breezes. The open road before him. Not a care in the world.

"*Oh, I do like to be beside the seaside,*" he sang out in a burst of sheer joy.

Sam Thrums began to sing, too, in a tuneless voice as he trudged along the road.

"*There was a wee cooper who lived in Fife.*
Nickety-nackety-noo-noo-noo."

Macpherson tried to whistle the tune but they were never on the same note together. All the while the junk-man kept a sharp look-out for second-hand goods. He seemed to know by instinct where he could find them.

"Up here!" he shouted suddenly. "*Nickety-nackety-noo-noo-noo.*"

He turned the pony's head and led the way along a narrow lane to a little cottage where he knocked at the door. An old woman with a shawl round her shoulders came out.

"Scrap?" said she, when Sam spoke to her. "Ay,

you've come to the right place. Come away in and have a look.''

In a short time Sam came out carrying a broken bedstead. Into the cart it went, followed by an old clock, an armchair with no legs, and a couple of cracked vases.

"How did you know?" asked Macpherson, as they went jogging on their way.

"Oh, I can smell it out, young fellow-me-lad," said Sam, winking at the pony. And so he could! It was not long before the cart was piled up with old lamps, broken chairs, pails, jugs, ornaments, and even a battered old banjo. There was no room for Macpherson who was forced to get out and walk. But Maisie still sat amongst the clutter, with the pony's hat almost hiding her flushed, happy face.

They were jingling along a narrow road on their homeward journey when they saw a notice outside a cottage. FRESH EGGS FOR SALE.

"Hold on!" cried Sam Thrums, and went up to the cottage door. He came back carrying a little basket of eggs. "A wee present for your auntie," he said, handing the basket to Macpherson. "You wait, young fellow-me-lad! I'll get her to ride in my cart before long. Sam Thrums never fails. Here! you'd better carry them carefully. They'll get broken if you dump them in the cart."

Macpherson knew only too well about the danger of breaking eggs. How often had Old Skinflint warned him not to shoogle them? So he took the basket and carried it as carefully as he could.

Little did he know how soon the eggs would all be smashed to smithereens.

5

Accident!

Macpherson walked along beside the pony, thinking dreamily about the sea and the lighthouse but not forgetting to carry the basket of eggs carefully. Perhaps Aunt Janet would boil one for his tea when he got home; and Grandpa, too, would enjoy their fresh taste. Maisie Murphy, without doubt, would find a way of sharing their meal. She had already announced that she was "thtarving".

"Oh, I do like to be. . . ."

Macpherson had no sooner started to sing than he heard a zooming sound behind him and a warning shout from Sam Thrums.

"Look out, young fellow-me-lad! Jump for it."

The only place to jump was into the ditch. Macpherson landed in a clump of nettles, with egg-yolk and cracked shells all around him.

"Mercy me!" he gasped in dismay, gazing at the wreckage. Then, as the zooming sound came closer, he glanced up and saw a red sports-car flash past.

The piebald pony reared himself up on his

hind legs and gave a whinny of alarm as the car whizzed past him. Maisie, too, gave a shriek as she tumbled backwards in amongst the broken bedsteads and old pails. The banjo gave a twang, as if in protest, and Sam rushed forward to catch the reins so that he could soothe the startled pony.

"Whoa! Steady, Soapsuds, steady!" Sam's face was red with rage. "It's that young Lord from the Beach Hotel," he burst out, shaking his fist at the disappearing car. "He thinks that the whole world belongs to him." He patted the pony, hauled Maisie upright, and then looked over his shoulder at Macpherson. "Are you all right, young fellow-me-lad?"

"Y-Yes," said Macpherson, emerging from the ditch, rubbing the nettle-stings from his bare legs. "But I'm sorry the eggs are broken." Not to mention the basket, which was squashed to pulp. Mr McGlashan, the grocer, would have killed him!

Sam Thrums was different. "Not to worry," said the junk-man, recovering his good humour. "I'll give your auntie another present. Anything in the cart she might fancy, Miss Murphy?"

Maisie prinked herself up. She liked being addressed as Miss Murphy. Settling the pony's hat more firmly on her head, she began to rummage amongst the goods Sam had collected. She discarded the banjo, the bedsteads, the dented pails, and the cracked jugs.

"What about thith?" She pulled out a fat teapot with pictures of roses all around it, even on the spout, and not a crack to be seen.

"The very thing!" Sam Thrums winked at Macpherson. "She makes a good cup of tea, does your auntie. And this is bigger than the one at Sea View. I like three cups." The junk-man smacked his lips and went on his way, singing, "*Nickety-nackety-noo-noo-noo*."

Macpherson followed on. His legs were still smarting from the nettle-stings, but that was nothing compared with the joy of being out in the open with the sun shining and the smell of salt sea in the air.

"*O, I do like to be....*"

They were almost home. Round the next bend they would be in sight of Sea View.

"I'm thtarving," said Maisie Murphy. Then, as the cart rattled round the corner, she swayed in her seat and let out a startled scream. Her chubby cheeks went pale. "Oh Macpherthon!" she cried in a shaky voice. "Look!"

Macpherson ran forward and to his horror saw the tangled wreckage of the red sports-car lying in a crumpled heap at the roadside. Beside it lay the young man, as still as death.

Later that day there were two wheel-chairs parked outside the door of Sea View. Grandpa's old one and the Duchess's shiny new one. Cinderella's pram was there, too, and the piebald pony was tethered to the newly-mended gate.

Inside the little house there was scarcely room to turn. Aunt Janet's face was flushed, and no wonder. It was not every day she entertained a real Duchess to tea. The others were all there, too, crowded round the table, except the Murphy baby, who lay on the rug, sucking her thumb.

It was as well that Aunt Janet had been presented with the fat teapot, for everyone was clamouring for second cups. Or third, in the case of Sam Thrums, who was not in the least put out by the presence of such a fine lady as the Duchess.

She was sitting at the top of the table in the place of honour, holding a teacup in her thin, frail hand.

"Are you feeling better now, Duchess?" asked Grandpa, looking anxiously at her pale face.

"Yes, thank you." She smiled faintly at him and at Aunt Janet, then took a little sip from the cup. "You have been most kind. This tea is reviving me."

"Ay, she makes a good brew, does the lassie," said Sam Thrums heartily. He reached across for a home-made pancake. "She's not a bad baker either. Or a bad looker, if she would just give us a smile now and again."

Aunt Janet tossed her head and said sharply to Maisie, "Is that your third pancake, Maisie Murphy?"

"Yeth, it ith," confessed Maisie; "but I'm not full yet."

"It's the fresh air," said Grandpa, beaming at her. "Why not have a scone and jam, Maisie my dear? It'll fill up the odd corners."

While Maisie's odd corners were being filled the others sat back and relaxed over their final cups of tea.

"He'll be all right," Grandpa said to the Duchess, seeing the little frown of worry gathering on her brow. "You know what the hospital doctor said. No need to worry."

She nodded her head with its dainty lace cap on top. "Yes, I know. I ought to be grateful that things are not worse." She sighed and said, "Poor darling Ronald!" Then she turned to Macpherson. "Thank you for all you have done."

"Oh, it was nothing, ma'am."

But it was Macpherson who had sped off to the Cottage Hospital to raise the alarm and fetch an ambulance. And it was Macpherson who had run all the way to the Beach Hotel to break the news of the accident to the Duchess.

The old lady was sitting in her wheel-chair under a shady tree in the hotel grounds. Her little granddaughter, Lady Sarah, sat on the grass nearby making a daisy-chain with the help of her stout, red-faced nanny. When Macpherson ran past them, the woman rose up and called out angrily, "What are you doing here, boy? Go away! This is a private hotel."

The little girl dropped her daisy-chain and cried "Oh Nanny! it's that boy we met on the and. I'd like to speak to him. . . ."

But Macpherson had gone straight to the old lady, who looked up at him in surprise and said in her sweet voice, "Why, hullo Macpherson, how nice to see you again. Come and sit beside me and tell me all about. . . ."

"There's been an accident, ma'am," said Macpherson breathlessly.

"An accident!" All the colour drained from her face. "It's Ronald! My poor darling boy! He's dead!"

"No, no, ma'am!" said Macpherson hastily. "It's only his leg. He was out in his car. . . ."

"I knew it!" she cried, trying to rise from her wheel-chair. "Where is he? I must go to him at once. My poor boy!"

"I'll take you," said Macpherson, settling her back in her chair. "He's at the Cottage Hospital. Don't worry, ma'am. The doctor says he'll be O.K."

The doctor had said a great deal more than that! That sports-cars, carelessly driven, were a menace on the roads. That the young man was lucky to be alive. That he would have to lie still for weeks and learn patience.

"Patience!" sighed the Duchess as Macpherson wheeled her away from the Cottage Hospital. "Poor darling Ronald, he'll be *so* bored."

"Maybe it'll do him good," said Macpherson wisely. He looked at the old lady's white face. "What you need, ma'am, is a cup of tea."

"Oh Macpherson, how did you guess?" she said faintly. "But where could we have it?"

"Here," said Macpherson, wheeling the chair straight towards Sea View.

So here they all were making good use of the fat teapot and enjoying Aunt Janet's home-baking. There was so much lively chatter that the Duchess began to forget her troubles. The colour came back to her cheeks, and everything that was said seemed to amuse her.

"I don't know when I have enjoyed myself so much," she declared happily. Then she remembered the accident. "If it was not for that poor boy lying in the hospital. . . ."

"He'll soon be better, Duchess," Grandpa assured her. "We'll all go and visit him, and Macpherson will take you any time you like. Isn't that so, my old shipmate?"

"Ay, ay, Captain."

Grandpa pushed back his chair and picked up his latest treasure. It was not only Aunt Janet who had received a present from Sam Thrums. The old man was now the proud possessor of a telescope which had seen better days.

"But wait till I've polished it up a bit," said Grandpa, and began there and then to give it a rub with a soft duster. True enough, before long it began to sparkle like silver.

"First-rate!" Grandpa held it up to the light and peered through the lens. "Ship-shape! I can see that horse of yours, Mr Thrums, at the gate. Shiver my timbers! he looks as big as an elephant. And what's that passing by? An enormous donkey."

"Thilly-Willy," said Maisie, looking over his shoulder. "Mungo'th taking him home to the thtable."

Sam Thrums rose to his feet. "Time I was away, too." He bowed politely to the Duchess, then turned to Aunt Janet ."Thanks for the tea, lassie. Remember, my carriage awaits you any time you fancy. Sam Thrums is always at your service."

The lassie, trying hard to curb her tongue in front of the Duchess, bit back a sharp reply and gave the junk-man one of her hard looks instead. He grinned back at her, then said to Macpherson, "Before I forget, young fellow-me-lad, it's tomorrow."

"What's tomorrow?" asked Macpherson.

"The lighthouse. I'm taking some supplies out to Davy. So you can come with me, if you like."

Macpherson's face went pink with pleasure. "Oh yes, Mr Thrums, I like!" He was so delighted he could have flung his arms round Sam's neck.

Instead he said excitedly to Grandpa, "Did you hear that, Grandpa? I'm going to the lighthouse."

The old man turned his telescope on him and said, "Good for you, shipmate. I'll watch you from the shore. It'll be almost as good as going there myself."

"Oh, Macpherthon, can't I come, too?" asked Maisie, swallowing her last piece of jammy scone.

To Macpherson's relief Sam Thrums shook his head and answered for him. "Not this time, Miss Murphy. No room in the boat."

Miss Murphy's lower lip began to quiver. Great tears ran down her cheeks like raindrops. She could turn them on quickly, but luckily they never lasted for long. When the Duchess spoke to her she wiped them away and was all smiles in an instant.

"Why not come and visit me, my dear, at the Beach Hotel? Tomorrow at teatime."

"Teatime! Oh yeth! I will. Thankth!" Tea with the Duchess at her grand hotel! It would be even better than going to the lighthouse.

"My little granddaughter, Sarah, would love to play with you, my dear. She's a very lonely child. It's her nanny's afternoon off."

"Oh, good!" said Maisie, recalling her encounter with the severe woman. "Will there be bunth?" she asked.

"Bunth?" said the Duchess in a puzzled voice. "For tea."

"Oh yes, buns," said the Duchess, smiling at her. "Lots of them. With pink icing."

Maisie sighed with satisfaction. "Then that'th O.K.," she said, and went to pick up the baby from the rug. She had something to look forward to. And so had Macpherson.

That night he could scarcely sleep for excitement. Time and again he climbed out of bed, stood on the chair and peered out of the skylight window. Yes! it was still there, the lighthouse, winking at him as if to say, "I'm here, Macpherson, waiting for you. See you tomorrow."

Next day it rained. Not just a dribble. A real downpour.

"Sea View!" grumbled Aunt Janet, gazing dismally out into the dripping garden. "Some view! I can hardly see as far as the gate."

"It'll freshen the flowers," said Grandpa cheerfully.

But would it prevent Macpherson from going to the lighthouse?

"Not a bit, my old shipmate," Grandpa assured him. "Sam Thrums is not the fellow to be put off by a few showers. But you'd best hunt around and see if you can find some wet-weather gear."

"You'll get drowned," said Aunt Janet, as Macpherson searched in the cupboard under the stairs. "Remember, I warned you."

"Yes, I'll remember, Aunt Janet," promised Macpherson, hauling out an old set of oilskins and a pair of big gum-boots which had once belonged to Miss Peacock's cousin.

"Try them on for size, my boy," said Grandpa. Then: "Blow me down! he must have been a giant, old Hector. Where are you, Macpherson?"

"I'm here, Grandpa," said Macpherson, pushing back his waterproof hat. He was almost swamped by the oilskins, which were much too long and much too wide for him. But at least they would keep him dry.

"What's all the hurry?" asked Aunt Janet, as he pulled on his seven-league boots. "It'll be hours yet before that Thrums man comes."

"I've got something else to do first," said Macpherson, tottering towards the door. "I'm going to visit the young Lord at the hospital. I promised the Duchess."

He went out into the garden and picked a bunch of wet roses. Then he strode off to the Cottage Hospital in his big boots.

6

The Lighthouse at Last

"I can't see it," said Macpherson, peering through the driving rain in the direction of the lighthouse. "Are we getting nearer, Mr Thrums?"

"Near enough, young fellow-me-lad. Hold on till I get my bearings."

Sam Thrums's motor-boat was every bit as creaky as his junk-cart. Leaky, too. Macpherson had a feeling that he would soon be bailing out. The sea beyond the harbour was choppy. At any moment the waves might swamp the boat. But it was an adventure, all the more thrilling because of the spice of danger.

Sam Thrums took it all in his stride. In between singing "*Nickety-nackety-noo-noo-noo*" at the top of his voice, he kept up a running conversation with Macpherson.

"How was the young Lord, then? At the hospital."

"Fed up."

"What? Already! Wait till he has been there for another week or two. If you ask me, he's lucky to be alive. Silly young . . ."

The rest of his words were whipped away with the wind. Macpherson huddled under his oilskins and thought back to his morning visit to the Cottage Hospital. The young Lord had been none too pleased to see him. Neither were the nurses when he came in out of the rain, carrying the dripping roses in his hand.

"Take off those oilskins," said a starched Sister severely, outside the door of the patient's private room. "And don't stay too long. Lord Ronald must rest."

The young Lord was lying in bed near the window, staring out at the rain with a peevish expression on his face.

"Hullo," said Macpherson, standing on one leg and hiding the flowers behind his back. He was not sure what to say or how to say it. "How – er – how are you?"

The young man turned his gaze on Macpherson but did not seem to find him any more pleasant a sight than the rain.

"The Macpherson boy," he said in a bored voice. "What are you doing here?"

"I just came to see you," said Macpherson, shifting to the other foot. "I brought you some roses."

"Roses!" said the young Lord irritably. "Don't wave them about like that. Put them down."

Macpherson laid the flowers on the bedside table and stood back. The conversation had come to a full stop. Lord Ronald was turning his head away and closing his eyes as if he did not want to see or hear any more. But Macpherson stubbornly stood his ground. Now that he was here, he was determined to make his presence felt. Perhaps he could relieve the young man's boredom by talking to him.

"Your grandmother – er – the Duchess sends her love. She's coming to see you soon. So is Grandpa, and Maisie Murphy. She's here on her holidays, too. From Glasgow. That's where we all live, in one of the high-rise flats up near the sky. We get a great view, but of course, it's better here at the seaside. D'you know what? I'm going to visit the lighthouse this afternoon. Isn't it exciting?"

No response. But Macpherson did not give up. He went on to tell about Sam Thrums and Silly-Willy, about Old Skinflint, the grocer, about life in the Glasgow streets, and the fun he and Grandpa had making ships-in-bottles. Anything and everything he could think of to take the listless young man's mind off his own troubles.

The patient kept his eyes closed, but Macpherson thought he could detect a faint flicker of interest on the man's face. And when a nurse came in, saying sharply, "Time's up," Lord Ronald turned his head and opened his eyes wide.

"Come again," he said, looking straight at Macpherson.

The boy smiled to himself as he went out into the rain. His visit had not been in vain, after all!

Would the visit to the lighthouse be as successful, or would they be forced to turn back? A spray of ice-cold sea-water splashed against Macpherson's face, causing him to gasp and splutter. The engine, too, spluttered, as the boat swerved and came to a shuddering stop.

"We're here, young fellow-me-lad," cried Sam Thrums, dashing the spray from his face. "Look, the lighthouse!"

There it was, looming up out of the mist, standing firmly on its rocky base with great, frothy waves breaking all around it. The lighthouse at last!

Macpherson felt a surge of excitement. Soon he would be inside. But how? There was not a sign of life. Only a seagull or two screaming with rage as they flew off through the drenching rain.

Suddenly a door opened near the base of the lighthouse and Macpherson caught sight of a red weather-beaten face. A giant of a man appeared, calling out, "Ahoy there, Sam!" in a voice that rose above the gale.

"Ahoy, Big Davy! Catch the rope."

The lighthouse-keeper stretched out his powerful arms and caught the rope in a firm grasp. The boat tossed and turned as if trying to escape, but it was no match for the big man who soon had it safely moored by the side of the lighthouse.

"Out you go, young fellow-me-lad," said Sam Thrums, pushing Macpherson forward. "Davy'll catch you."

It seemed a perilous step for Macpherson to

take, with such an angry sea hissing around him. He took a deep breath, braced himself, and scrambled out on to the slippery rock. The next moment he felt himself gripped like a vice in the keeper's strong arms. He was safe.

"Steady, boy, steady!" boomed the big man. "You next, Sam."

But Sam, taking everything in his stride, had already leapt on to the rock, lugging a large sack of supplies behind him. And now they were inside, with the door firmly shut.

Macpherson's dream had come true.

"Isn't it great!" he gasped, getting his breath back and trying to look in every direction at once. But all he could see was a winding staircase.

"Take off your oilskins and follow me," said Big Davy. "You'll be ready for a cup of tea. The kettle's on the boil."

Tea in a lighthouse! Just as if it was an ordinary household.

Macpherson thought of Maisie Murphy, dressed up in her cast-off finery, taking tea in style with the Duchess, doubtless with fancy cakes and the very best china. But what could be better than having tea in a lighthouse, whether the cups were cracked or not?

He followed the others up the winding staircase, round and round, up and up. Macpherson had an impression of shining brass, of polished wood-work, of everything being clean and sparkling. Now and again he had glimpses through the windows of the stormy sea outside. Then all at once they were in a room, half-way up, as snug as the kitchen at Sea View. They had reached the keeper's living-quarters.

A silent man was sitting at the table, mending a sock.

"That's Joe, my assistant," said Big Davy. He shouted at the man. "Joe! Visitors! Here's my brother Sam; and this is Macpherson, from Glasgow."

The man looked up and nodded, then went on mending his sock without saying a word.

"He's not much of a talker," said the keeper, pouring boiling water into a brown teapot. "But he's a great baker, is Joe." He pushed forward a platter of freshly-made scones and another of golden-brown pancakes. "Help yourself," he said to Macpherson. "You'll have to eat them as they are. We've run short of butter and jam."

"No, you haven't," grinned Sam Thrums, opening out his sack of supplies. "See! Butter, jam, tea, eggs, sausages, cheese, flour, tobacco. . . ."

The silent man looked up and seemed suddenly to have come to life. He laid aside his darning and brought an empty pipe from his pocket.

"Ah! that's what Joe's been missing. Baccy!" said Sam, handing a packet to the man. "There you are, Joe, my boy. Now you can smoke to your heart's content."

Joe still said nothing, only nodded his thanks and filled his pipe. He struck a match to light it and let out a great puff of smoke. Then he went back to his darning with a more contented look on his face.

Meanwhile Macpherson was doing justice to his tea. The stormy journey across the sea had sharpened his appetite, and one by one the scones and pancakes were vanishing from the platters.

"They're good!" he told Joe. "Do you always do the cooking?"

Joe puffed at his pipe and gave a grunt which might have meant Yes. It was Big Davy who answered for him.

"Ay, he's a handy man is our Joe. Always dusting and polishing. Baking and cooking. Keeping the place as clean as a new pin."

Joe gave another grunt and bent his head lower over his darning, while Macpherson took an interested look around him. It was true, there was not a speck of dust to be seen, nor a thing out of place. Yet, in spite of its neatness, there was a homely air about the little living-room. Shelves of books, photographs on the wall, china ornaments, cushions, even a vase filled with artificial flowers.

"Where do you sleep?" Macpherson wanted to know.

"Next door," Big Davy told him. "Come and have a look."

The big man had to duck his head as he went through to the next room where the bunks were placed. They were neatly-made and snug-looking. What would it be like, Macpherson wondered, to sleep out here in the middle of the raging sea with the waves lashing around the lighthouse and no other human beings within sight?

He was soon to find out!

The keeper took him on a tour of inspection, past the store-room, the fog-signal room, the control-room, and finally to the light-room at the very top.

This was the most exciting place of all, where the revolving lights sent out their signals from small reflecting lenses. The lights Macpherson could see from his bedroom at Sea View.

On the way up Big Davy explained the working of the lighthouse; but there was so much to take in that it all became confused in Macpherson's mind. He tried hard to remember it so that he could tell it to Grandpa later on, but the details became all merged and muddled.

"Of course, a lot of it is automatic nowadays, lad," Big Davy was saying. "No lamps to light, but we must see that everything is in working-order and keep the lenses clean. There's never any letting-up in a lighthouse. We're always ready for an emergency. I'll take you down to the machine-room later on and show you how things work there. Any questions?"

There were a hundred questions Macpherson wanted to ask, but one above all. "Could I get out on that wee balcony, please?"

"In weather like this! You won't see anything, ad, and you'll have to hang on like grim death. But if you're sure."

"I'm sure," said Macpherson.

He wanted to get the real feeling of being sea-bound on a lighthouse, with the lashing waves below and the stormy sky above. He could see it all through the window, but out on the balcony he would really be in the thick of it.

The moment Big Davy opened the door Macpherson's breath was taken away. Not only by the gusting wind and the driving rain, but by the magnificence of the scene. He clung on tightly to the rail with one hand and rubbed the rain from his eyes with the other, trying to see everything that lay around him. Great foaming waves chased each other, faster and faster, across the open sea,

as if they were running a desperate race. When they broke around the base of the lighthouse the spray was flung high into the air, falling back to the sea like a fountain of white froth. It was a sight Macpherson would never forget.

"Mercy me! It's great!" he gasped. He could find no other words to convey his feelings. But this was not a time for speech, with the wind buffeting at him from all directions and the rain lashing against his face. Perched up so high, he felt part of the elements himself, at one with the wind and the rain and the sea.

But the sky had suddenly darkened and Big Davy hastily pulled him back inside. There was a note of alarm in the keeper's voice when he spoke.

"Inside, lad! It's not safe. We'll have to set the fog-horn going." He looked anxiously at the sky and shook his head. "There'll be no chance of you getting back to shore tonight. You'll have to stay in the lighthouse."

On shore, little Miss Murphy was having the time of her life. So was the Duchess, seated beside her at a little tea-table in the lounge of the Beach Hotel, laughing merrily at Maisie's lively conversation.

On a dais in the corner an orchestra was playing soft music. Rose-coloured curtains were drawn to blot out the dull day. The shaded lights, the tinkle of tea-cups, the sweet-smelling flowers, the music – all had gone to young Maisie's head. On top of it was perched her best Jumble Sale hat with yet another artificial rose added to the brim. Her cheeks were flushed, her eyes sparkled, and for once she had had her fill of good things to eat. Dainty sandwiches, wafer-thin bread-and-butter, little buns with coloured icing on top, chocolate fingers, and a sponge-cake oozing with fresh cream

"I'm full," she said, sitting back with a replete

sigh. "Thankth for the tea, Your Grathe. It wath thplendid."

"You're looking splendid yourself," smiled Her Grace. "I *have* enjoyed your visit, Masie, my dear, and so has little Sarah. You've done us a lot of good."

Indeed, the only one who had not enjoyed Maisie's visit was Mrs Crump. Little Lady Sarah's nanny had shown her disapproval at the outset. When the Duchess suggested that the two children might play together in the hotel games-room, Mrs Crump's red face grew redder with anger.

"It's too wet outside," said the Duchess. "Afterwards Maisie and I will have tea together, just by ourselves. Come along, Nanny, leave them alone. They'll get on better that way. And it's your afternoon off."

Mrs Crump tossed her head. "Begging your pardon, Your Grace," she said, as the two young things ran off together, "I don't think that Murphy child is the right companion for our little Ladyship. Who knows what rough ways she might teach her?"

"Nonsense, Nanny. It's time Sarah learned a little rough-and-tumble. It'll do her good. Come along; let them enjoy themselves in their own way."

They did! True, her little Ladyship's frock was

torn and her hair tousled by the time the two had romped together for an hour. Her hands and face were dirty, her knees were scratched, but there was no doubt she had enjoyed herself thoroughly. There was more colour in her cheeks, more sparkle in her eyes. And she had learned two new skills. How to turn somersaults and how to lisp!

"Oh Maithie! what fun it'th been!" she cried when Mrs Crump came to collect her. "Mutht I go, Nanny?"

"Yes, you must. And stop talking in that ridiculous way," said Mrs Crump crossly. She turned to Maisie, her face bright red with anger. "Look what you've done to her! What a state she's in, poor child. She won't sleep tonight; she's far too over-excited. Come along at once, Lady Sarah. Bath and bed."

"Wait," said her little Ladyship, turning back to Maisie. "You haven't told me about that boy. Where is he?"

"Macpherthon? He'th out in the lighthouthe. He'll thoon be back and we can play on the thandth another day. And you can ride Thilly-Willy again. Ta-ta, Lady Tharah."

"Ta-ta, Maithie."

They were friends for life!

"You must come again, my dear," the Duchess said, smiling at Maisie across the tea-table.

"Oh yeth, I will!"

"And please go and visit poor darling Ronald at the hospital. If anyone can cheer him up, you will! Now, Maisie, my dear, since it's so wet, I'm going to send you home in my car."

It was the biggest car Maisie had ever seen, driven by a chauffeur in smart uniform, who touched his cap before helping her in. As it purred smoothly along the promenade Maisie sat bolt upright on the soft cushions and peered out of the window, hoping that someone would recognize her. It was a pity it was raining so hard and there were so few people about. She would have liked to have bowed and waved, as the Queen did. But there was only one solitary figure plodding on his way through the downpour, carrying a heavy shopping-bag.

"It'th Mungo, the donkey-boy!" Maisie rapped on the partition in front of her and called to the chauffeur. "Thtop! could you pleathe give him a lift?"

7

A Surprise Visit

The donkey-boy looked up in surprise when the shining car purred to a stop beside him and the chauffeur touched his cap in salute.

"Get in, Mungo," said Maisie, helping him with his bundles. "Where have you been and where ith Thilly-Willy?"

"He's in the stable," said Mungo, stumbling in beside her. "It's too wet today for donkey-rides, so I've been doing some shopping for the old gent at Sea View."

"Grandpa! Good!" said Maisie. "We'll thtop there. Thettle down, Mungo, and enjoy the ride. Ithn't thith great?"

Mungo sat on the edge of his seat, goggle-eyed at all the luxury. It was a pity the ride was so short. All too soon they reached the gate of Sea View and once more Maisie rapped on the partition.

"Thtop, pleathe. We're here."

Aunt Janet was boiling eggs for tea when they went in.

"Wipe your feet," she said sharply. Then she

gave Maisie one of her hard looks and said, "*You* won't be needing a boiled egg. I expect you ate plenty at that grand hotel."

"Yeth, I did," admitted Maisie. She looked longingly at the eggs bubbling in the pan. "But I might manage one. And Mungo'll be thtarving."

Grandpa gave a chuckle. "Put in some more eggs, Janet woman. Young things are always hungry." He took the shopping-bag from Mungo and said, "Thanks, my boy; you've saved us a long trail in the rain. Come near the fire and get yourself dry."

Mungo went and sat on the rug before the cheerful fire. It was not often that the donkey-boy found himself in such cosy surroundings. This was a real home – not a draughty stable – with the kettle singing and Aunt Janet making toast for tea. Perhaps it would stifle him to live always in such a confined space. But today, with the rain battering against the window-pane, it seemed the most comfortable place on earth.

He gave a sigh of content and was half-asleep when Aunt Janet said, "Sit in to the table". In spite of her sharpness she saw that he had enough to eat. Two boiled eggs, plenty of buttered toast, and a large slice of her home-made apple-pie.

Maisie had finished eating her one egg and had helped herself to a piece of apple-pie when a bluster of wind rattled the rain against the window.

"Ithn't it thtormy?" she said, peering out at the angry sky. "I wonder how Macpherthon'th getting on?"

It was then that they heard the first sound of the fog-signal. Boom! Boom! Boom!

"Shiver my timbers!" said Grandpa, sitting up straight.

"What'th that?" said Maisie, in alarm.

Boom! Boom! Boom!

"Trouble!" cried Aunt Janet, with the flowery teapot poised in her hand. "I knew it! That Sam Thrums should have had more sense than take Macpherson out in weather like this. They'll both be drowned, you mark my words."

Boom! Boom! Boom!

Maisie's lip began to tremble and she put the apple-pie back on the plate. Her appetite had gone.

"Oh dear! what can we do to thave them?" she cried, turning to Grandpa in distress. Tears flooded her eyes and began to drip down her chubby cheeks. Then suddenly she brushed them away and jumped to her feet. "I know! Mungo and I'll go out in the lifeboat and get them."

"Sit down, Maisie my dear," said Grandpa calmly. "Sam will know what to do. If it's too stormy he and Macpherson will stay in the lighthouse till the weather clears. There's nothing to worry about. It'll be an adventure for Macpherson. I can't wait till my old shipmate comes back and tells us all about it."

"Well, if you thay tho, Grandpa," said Maisie, looking less troubled. But the booming sound still worried her, and the apple-pie remained uneaten.

Grandpa was right. It was an adventure for Macpherson.

The only thing that worried him was Grandpa himself. "I wonder if he'll hear the signal and know what's happening?" he said to Sam Thrums.

" 'Course he'll know, an old sea-dog like your Grandpa," Sam assured him. Then he gave a chuckle and winked at Macpherson. "I'm not so sure about your auntie. *She*'ll have something to say! Still, I'll get round her yet, you wait and see."

The two of them were alone in the keeper's living quarters. Big Davy and Joe had gone about their business. At the first hint of danger the silent man had suddenly sprung to life, as if he had been wound up. He was here, there, and everywhere. Down in the engine-room, up to the light-room, peering out into the darkness, listening and looking to see that all was well. Now and again he stopped on the way through to prepare a concoction for their evening meal. But still he remained silent.

"All O.K., Joe?" Sam Thrums asked him.

The man nodded, gave a stir to the pot, and was off again on his rounds.

Meantime the fog-signal sounded solemnly over the sea. It was an eerie noise at such close quarters. Macpherson tried to peer out of the window, but there was nothing to see except the faint light from above shimmering on the water. Were there any ships in distress out there, he wondered?

Boom! Boom! Boom!

"Is there nothing we can do?" he asked Sam Thrums, anxious to help.

"Yes, there is. Keep out of the way, young fellow-me-lad, and lay the table for supper. I'll fry some sausages to go with that stuff of Joe's in the pot. Whatever it is."

Whatever it was had a very appetising smell as it bubbled away on the side of the stove. So had Sam's sausages when they started to sizzle in the frying-pan.

Big Dave sniffed hungrily as he came in, and slumped down in a chair.

"Good! Let's have supper. We can take a breather now. Joe! Come and dish up."

Joe came in and gave a final stir to the mysterious pot. Then he examined the contents closely and gave a grunt of satisfaction.

"Joe's speciality!" said Big Davy in an aside.

"Fills up the odd corners." He speared a couple of sausages from the frying-pan and held out his plate. The silent man dished out generous helpings, scraping the bottom of the pot so that no morsel was wasted. Then he stood back and waited.

"Very tasty," said Sam Thrums, smacking his lips. "Very tasty indeed!"

"Great!" agreed Macpherson. Never before had he tasted such a savoury mixture of potatoes, onions, and herbs, which went so well with the fried sausages that soon every plate was scraped clean, and there was a look of satisfaction on Joe's face as he sat back and filled his pipe.

For a time they all relaxed, while Big Davy told tales of being storm-stayed for weeks in the lighthouse, and how Joe had once broken his leg and had to be taken off by helicopter, and of the night when a foreign vessel foundered on the rocks and they rescued the crew.

"Couldn't make out a word they said. Strangely enough, it was Joe here who acted as go-between, and you know how seldom *he* speaks." The keeper threw back his head and laughed at the memory of it. Then he pulled himself together and jumped up. "Come along, Joe. We'd better do the rounds again." He looked at Macpherson whose head was beginning to nod. "As for you, lad, you'd better bunk down. You'll remember your first visit to a lighthouse?"

"I'll never forget it," said Macpherson, trying to rub the sleep from his eyes. "It's been great!"

He tried his best to keep awake in his bunk long enough to savour the exciting feeling of being marooned out at sea. But his eyelids kept closing. Boom! Boom! Boom! . . . he was drifting away into a sound sleep.

"Yoo-hoo, Macpherthon! Welcome back! Look, Thinderella, there he ith, in the boat," cried Maisie Murphy, prancing about at the edge of the sea.

During the night the storm had blown itself out. By morning the sky was blue, the sun shone, and the sea was as still as a mill-pond.

The motor-boat with Macpherson and Sam Thrums on board was nearing the beach where Maisie was waiting, with the Murphy baby crooning in the pram beside her. Grandpa was there, too, strolling along the sand on his shaky pins. Not so shaky now! The old sea-dog was gaining strength every day. "I'll be riding Silly-Willy before long," he called out to Mungo, who was doing a roaring trade now that the sunshine had brought out the holiday-makers again.

The other donkey-boys were busy enough, too;

so for once there was no rivalry between them. In any case, they were not likely to cause trouble with Miss Maisie Murphy's watchful eye on them!

Little Lady Sarah was waiting her turn to ride Silly-Willy, with her hand clutched tightly by her Nanny. Mrs Crump was reluctant to let her small charge go, after what happened last time. But the Duchess, sitting watching in her wheel-chair on the promenade, had given her permission.

"Let the child have a treat, Nanny. She'll come to no harm, and I'll enjoy watching her cantering along the sea-shore."

So her little Ladyship had her way. When her turn came Mungo helped her up on to the donkey's back, and Silly-Willy set off at a dancing-pace. Forward, sideways, backwards, round and round, as if he was waltzing.

Lady Sarah squealed with delight. "Oh, Nanny, isn't this fun? I *am* enjoying myself. Gee-up, Silly-Willy."

Mrs Crump frowned anxiously as she marched by the donkey's side. Her face grew redder when Silly-Willy threw up his head and gave a loud "Ee-haw!" as if he was laughing at her. Just then the motor-boat reached the shore, and everyone – including the donkey – rushed forward to welcome the occupants.

"Look out!" cried Mrs Crump. "You'll get

soaked." But Lady Sarah slithered off the donkey's back in time and landed laughing on the sand.

"That'th better," said Maisie, picking her up. "Jutht laugh. Don't cry." Her little Ladyship was learning!

Meantime Macpherson was back on dry land. He took a long look at the lighthouse, standing serene and solid out at sea, then he ran off to tell Grandpa all about his adventures.

Later that day Macpherson had one of the strangest surprises of his life.

He had run messages for Aunt Janet; he had weeded the garden, visited the young Lord at the hospital ("Come again soon, Macpherson," he had pleaded); he had wheeled Grandpa's chair down to the promenade, and now he was free to enjoy himself.

He was building a lighthouse of his own on the sand, with the help – or hindrance – of Maisie Murphy, who had insisted on lending him a hand. He had already built a little sand-crèche for Cinderella, who was lying in it nearby, kicking her bare heels in the air. So, with the baby safe, Maisie was free.

"You're awful clever, Macpherthon," she said, admiring the lighthouse as it rose higher and higher.

"Clever! I'm brilliant!" grinned Macpherson. "Keep out of the way, Maisie Murphy. If you want to help, go and collect some shells."

"Oh yeth, I will."

Maisie trotted eagerly away, and for a time Macpherson was left in peace to continue his task. He was absorbed in his work, putting the finishing-touches to the topmost tower when Maisie rushed back. So suddenly that she tripped on a piece of slippery sea-weed, stumbled against the lighthouse and down it toppled in ruins, with all Macpherson's careful work wasted.

"Look what you've done, you silly thing!" he

cried angrily. Then he saw the look on her face. "What's up?"

"It'th him!" she gasped, taking refuge behind Macpherson.

"Him?" Macpherson looked up. Then he, too, gave a startled gasp. "Mercy me! I'm seeing things."

"No, you're not. It'th him all right." Maisie beat a hasty retreat. "I'm off to look after Thinderella."

Macpherson was left alone to face up to the man who was striding along the sand towards him. Someone whom he normally saw in the grocer's shop in Glasgow. Someone who always made him tremble at the knees. Old Skinflint himself! What on earth was he doing here at the seaside? Surely he had not come to drag his message-boy back to Glasgow, and the holiday only half-over?

"H-Hullo, Mr McG-Glashan," stammered Macpherson, standing to attention.

Old Skinflint peered over his spectacles and gave a grunt. "Huh! The message-boy! Wasting time as usual, I see. What are you up to?"

Macpherson looked guiltily at the heap of sand at his feet. "I was building a lighthouse."

"You haven't made a very good job of it," said the grocer, in his sarcastic way. "Is there nothing useful you can find to do?"

"Well . . ." began Macpherson. If he had been back home in Glasgow Old Skinflint would have made him scrub out the back-shop or sent him scurrying away with a heavy message-basket to take to one of his customers. Idleness was something Mr McGlashan could not bear. But, after all, thought Macpherson defiantly, I'm on my holidays. He said it out loud. "I'm on my holidays."

"Holidays!" Old Skinflint took a look at the sea as if he hated the sight of it. "Waste of time."

Then what was he doing here?

"Have you – er – shut the shop?" Macpherson ventured to ask.

"Shut the shop!" Old Skinflint looked as if he was about to explode. "Certainly not." The very idea! "It's a half-holiday in Glasgow."

"Oh, so it is," said Macpherson, remembering. How could he have been silly enough to imagine that Mr McGlashan would have shut the shop on an ordinary working-day? But what had made him do such an unusual thing as take a trip to the seaside?

"Cheap excursion," muttered the grocer, looking a trifle shame-faced. "It was Miss Peacock . . ."

"Miss Peacock!" cried Macpherson. "Is *she* here? Where?"

"There," grunted Old Skinflint, pointing to the sea.

And there she was, bobbing about in the water like a plump porpoise, in a striped bathing-suit.

"Macpherson!" she called, catching sight of him and splashing her way out of the sea.

"Miss Peacock!" cried Macpherson, running to meet her. Fancy seeing her in a bathing-suit instead of a shop overall! Miss Peacock, his fairy godmother, who had worked so many miracles on his behalf! "But how on earth did you get *him* to come?"

"Oh, I have my methods," said Miss Peacock, wrapping herself in a fluffy towel. "He was getting grumpier than ever, so I thought a change of air might do him good. I can see it's agreeing with you, Macpherson. How are you enjoying yourself?"

"Tip-top! Thanks to you, Miss Peacock. I've done everything. I've been to the lighthouse. . . ."

"Hold on! Wait till I get dressed, then I'll come back with you to Sea View and hear all about everything. Won't be a jiffy," said Miss Peacock, hurrying off to a bathing-hut.

It was during the jiffy that Macpherson found himself face-to-face with Old Skinflint once more. Maisie was hiding in the crêche beside the baby and the grocer was plodding to and fro on the sand, casting a baleful look at the donkeys. Especially Silly-Willy, who was in one of his frisky moods.

"Stupid animal!" grunted Old Skinflint. "Why doesn't that boy keep him under control?" The grocer glared at Macpherson. "I tell you who he reminds me of. You! Stubborn, that's what he is. And you're the same."

It was high time, Macpherson thought, to change the subject. "Oh look!" he cried. "There's Grandpa and the Duchess waving."

"The Duchess?"

The grocer stopped in his tracks and took an interested look at the little old lady in the wheelchair beside Grandpa's. If there was one thing Mr McGlashan liked it was a title. Better still, a titled customer. It meant a great advertisement for his shop, as well as more money in his till. "Where does she live?" he asked with a greedy glint in his eye.

"She's here on holiday, but she lives in a big mansion-house on the outskirts of Glasgow," Macpherson told him. "She was saying she was thinking of changing her grocer," he went on craftily. Old Skinflint's bristly eyebrows began to twitch, and Macpherson knew that he had him! "Would you like to meet her, Mr McGlashan?"

"Yes, I would," Old Skinflint looked at Macpherson with a new respect, and for once he almost smiled. "Perhaps your holiday hasn't been such a waste of time, after all."

8

To the Rescue

It was certainly a day of surprises for Macpherson.

Who would have believed that he would be walking up the road side-by-side with Old Skinflint as if they were the best of friends?

But there were bigger surprises to come.

It was a strange procession. Macpherson was pushing Grandpa in his wheel-chair while Miss Peacock walked behind, giving a hand now and again to Maisie Murphy, trundling Cinderella in her battered old pram.

The grocer had a smug look on his face, like a cat who had been licking cream. He had met the Duchess! Not only that, she had smiled sweetly at him and held out a gloved hand for him to shake.

"Mr McGlashan! How do you do? I have heard all about you from Macpherson."

For a moment Old Skinflint was taken aback. He shot a suspicious glance at Macpherson, wondering what the young rascal had been saying about him. But his fears vanished when the Duchess went on in her soft voice, "I must come and visit your shop. It sounds just the place for me."

"Any time, Your Grace!" said the grocer eagerly. "You'll be very welcome. Very welcome indeed!"

He rubbed his hands and began mentally to count up the contents of his till. What a feather in his cap it would be! Almost like being patronized by royalty.

His step was lighter than usual as the little procession wended its way towards Sea View. Macpherson found it difficult to make conversation with him, but Grandpa did not turn a hair, and treated him as if he were an ordinary man.

"Nothing like the sea-breezes for putting a spot of colour in your cheeks. You're looking better already, Mr McGlashan. Why not get away from behind that counter of yours? You could buy a cottage by the sea-side. Or rent Miss Peacock's . . ."

"Grandpa!"

"What is it, my old shipmate?"

"Do you see what I see?" gasped Macpherson. For the second time that day he could not believe his eyes.

"Shiver my timbers!" said Grandpa, sitting bolt upright in his chair.

Trotting towards them came Soapsuds the pony, wearing his straw hat at a rakish angle. Sam Thrums was driving the creaky old junk-cart and grinning from ear to ear. Seated beside him was a familiar figure in her best hat and coat, and with an unusual rosy flush on her face.

"Aunt Janet! Goodness gracious!"

"What did I tell you, young fellow-me-lad?" cried Sam Thrums, drawing up at the gate. "Your auntie and I have been out for a spin. Very enjoyable it was, too. She's coming again tomorrow. Aren't you, m'dear?"

But Aunt Janet had closed up like a clam and not a word could be got out of her. Climbing hastily down from the cart she marched straight into the house without as much as a backward glance at the junk-man.

"Not to worry," grinned Sam Thrums, hitching up the reins. "Your auntie'll be back for more. Wait till tomorrow!"

But when tomorrow came the whole situation was changed. The weather once more took a turn for the worse, and so did Aunt Janet's spirits. Macpherson never found out what had made her go for a jaunt in the first place. Her lips were tightly pursed, and the subject was closed.

Indeed there had been little chance to discuss

anything in the confusion of Mr McGlashan's and Miss Peacock's visit. It was strange seeing Old Skinflint sitting relaxed in an armchair, accepting a fill of tobacco from Grandpa for his pipe. Macpherson could not get used to being at such close quarters with the grocer. At any moment he expected him to shout, "What's that message-boy doing? Look lively there! Don't stand about doing nothing, you lazy creature. I've a good mind to skin you alive!"

It was best, Macpherson thought, to keep out of his way. He went off upstairs to his little bedroom and stood on the rickety chair so that he could catch a glimpse of the lighthouse. What was Big Davy doing, he wondered? He tried to picture him, and Joe, too, going silently about his tasks or maybe baking scones for their tea.

"Macpherson! Are you there?" called Miss Peacock breathlessly.

She had climbed the stairs and was peering round the door into the little room. The house was familiar to her, for she had visited Sea View many times when her Cousin Hector was alive.

"That's what I used to do," she told Macpherson, when she came in. "Stand on the chair and look at the lighthouse! Jump down, Macpherson, and help me to rummage in the cupboard.

Cousin Hector used to keep a lot of old rubbish there. I was thinking of getting rid of some of it. Sam Thrums could maybe make use of it."

The sight Macpherson saw when she opened the wall-cupboard would certainly have made Sam jump for joy.

"Did you ever see such a collection of junk!" cried Miss Peacock.

But it was not all junk. Amongst the old oil lamps, cracked jugs, vases, brass ornaments, and broken dishes, there was one thing that made Macpherson's eyes sparkle when he saw it. It was a little silver replica of the lighthouse, complete in every detail. A miniature of the real thing.

Miss Peacock saw the look on his face.

"For you, Macpherson," she said, handing him the little lighthouse. "It'll remind you of your holiday at Sea View. The rest can go to Sam."

"Oh, Miss Peacock, you're a gem!"

Macpherson held the lighthouse lovingly in his hand. He would take it home with him to Glasgow and keep it on the shelf in his small bedroom in the skyscraper. Every time he looked at it he would smell the sea-breezes and imagine himself back in the real lighthouse.

Later on that night he went with Miss Peacock and Mr McGlashan to see them off on the excursion train. Miss Peacock was beaming brightly as she waved him good-bye, but Old Skinflint had reverted to his normal grumpy mood. Although he had enjoyed his trip to the seaside he would never admit it. Now he was thinking of the time and money he had wasted. It was all Miss Peacock's fault for persuading him. He glared at her and then at Macpherson, standing waving on the platform.

"You'll have to make up for all this gallivanting when you get back," he called crossly out of the window. "There'll be a lot extra to do in the shop, so you'd better be prepared to stir your stumps."

"Yes, I will, Mr McGlashan," promised Macpherson. As the train slid away, he added, "And I'll give your regards to the Duchess!"

It was a good parting shot, he felt!

Next day with the rain coming down in torrents Macpherson put on his oilskins and set off to the Cottage Hospital to visit the young Lord. He had nothing to take with him except the little silver lighthouse, which he put carefully in his pocket. Perhaps the patient would like to have a look at it.

He was surprised when he reached the room to hear the sound of merry laughter and cheerful voices from within. One of the voices was Maisie Murphy's.

Dressed in her draggled finery, Maisie was sitting on a chair by the bedside, doing her best to entertain the patient. And obviously succeeding.

"I've been telling the Lord a thtory," she informed Macpherson, gazing up at him with her big blue eyes.

"A very comical one," said the patient, throwing back his head and laughing at the thought of it. He looked much more lively and animated. His face was brighter and the peevish look had gone. Maisie's medicine had worked wonders. "You've certainly cheered me up. I don't know what I would have done without your visits."

"Would you like to thee me danthing?" Maisie offered. "I'm quite good." She got up, ready to pirouette around the room.

"You'd better not," said Macpherson, stopping her in time. "The nurses wouldn't like it. Look! what do you think of this?"

He pulled the little lighthouse out of his pocket and held it up for them to see.

"Just like the real thing," said the young man. "I tell you what, once I'm on my feet I'll take you out there in my speedboat. To the light-house."

"Oh, that would be great!" cried Macpherson. Then he remembered. "But we'll be away home in Glasgow by then."

Maisie's face fell. "Oh, tho we will."

"You can come back," said Lord Ronald cheerfully. "And don't forget, I'm coming to visit you in Glasgow." He turned to Macpherson. "I've promised Maisie to take her out for a run when I get my new racing-car."

"But you're not to drive too fatht or we'll *both* get broken legth," said Maisie severely. She was treating him like one of the Murphy children. "Now, you've got to be good. I've left a jig-thaw on the table. You can play with that, and I'll come and thee you tomorrow. Ta-ta, Lord!"

Macpherson and Maisie walked down the drive together in the rain. Maisie had a tattered umbrella which blew outside-in every few minutes. But she trudged on, her cheeks glowing as the wind whipped the colour into her face.

"We've done quite well," she said smugly. "The Lord'th getting better."

It was not his health she was talking about, Macpherson knew. True enough, the young man seemed to be showing more interest in others and thinking less of himself. Perhaps their visits *had* helped a little; but it would never do to let Maisie get above herself!

"Silly donkey!" he said, giving her a friendly nudge. They had reached her door by now and a cluster of Murphy children were peering out of the window watching for her return, with Murphy in his shirt-sleeves dandling the baby.

"Ta-ta, Macpherthon. What are you going to do now?" she asked, shaking the rain from her umbrella.

"Who knows? Something might happen."

It did!

As he went whistling away down the road in the rain towards Sea View, Macpherson heard a familiar clip-clop behind him and Sam Thrums's cheerful voice hailing him.

"Hullo, young fellow-me-lad. D'you reckon it'll be too wet for your auntie to come for a joy-ride?"

Macpherson brushed the raindrops from his face and looked up at the stormy sky.

"Yes, Mr Thrums, I reckon it will." But not too wet for *him*. "Where are you off to?" he asked hopefully.

"Promised to pick up some odds and ends at a cottage a mile or two along the shore road," said Sam, hoisting an old sack over his shoulders to keep out the rain. The pony, too, was wearing a protective covering – a waterproof cape that flapped around his body. His straw hat was sodden by now, but Soapsuds was still as frisky as ever, waggling his ears, whisking his tail, blowing down his nose and grinning broadly at Macpherson. "Like to come?"

"Oh, yes, please!"

Macpherson was up in the junk-cart in a twinkling. Sam Thrums handed him the reins and said, "You can drive, if you like, young fellow-me-lad. Steady does it. Straight ahead and along by the shore."

The waves were splashing up over the promenade. "Wouldn't like to be out in a boat on a day like this," said Sam, huddling under his sack. "Drive on, young fellow-me-lad. It'll do Soapsuds no harm to have a bath."

The pony pranced on, swerving to avoid a spray of sea-water. "Steady!" cried Macpherson, tugging at the reins. It was exciting to see the great waves rushing in to the shore and breaking against the rocks. What would it be like in the lighthouse? There would be no time today for Joe to bake his scones and pancakes.

In spite of the rough ride in the junk-cart Sam Thrums was sitting back half-asleep.

"Ay, she's good company," he said drowsily.

Macpherson thought the man was dreaming.

"Who?" he asked, keeping his eye on the wet road ahead.

"Your auntie," said Sam, opening his eyes. "Have you ever heard her singing?"

"Aunt Janet? No, never." The very idea!

"Sings like a linty. Knows all the old tunes, does your auntie. 'Just a Song at Twilight'. 'Home Sweet Home'. 'Two Lovely Black Eyes'. . . ."

"Mercy me!" Macpherson almost fell off the cart with surprise.

"You should have heard us singing duets! Ay, we make a great pair, me and your auntie."

He gave a chuckle and began humming one of the tunes. But not for long. Suddenly an explosion, like a sharp shot, cracked through the air. Then another and another, heard above the wailing of the wind and the splashing of the waves. At the sound, Soapsuds stopped dead in his tracks, cocked his ears, then did a right-about turn in the roadway.

"What's up?" shouted Macpherson, trying in vain to control the pony. Soapsuds had set off back along the coast road at such a smart pace that nothing would stop him.

"The rocket!" cried Sam, gathering himself together. "Ship in distress. Didn't I tell you, young fellow-me-lad, Soapsuds always recognizes the sound? He's off to the lifeboat."

It was a hair-raising journey, with the cart swaying from side to side and whirling round corners on one wheel. No use tugging at the reins. All Macpherson could do was cling on and hope that he would not be flung out.

As they neared the lifeboat, he had a feeling of mounting excitement, a mixture of fear and elation. There was danger in the air; adventure, too. But, of course, the most exciting adventure of all would be going out in the lifeboat. If only he could!

Soapsuds came to a sudden standstill, blowing down his nose and panting from his exertions. He had done his bit; now it was time for him to draw breath.

The crew were already gathering, tugging on oilskins and hurrying into life-jackets. They had come running from all directions, every man eager to get to his post. Mungo was amongst them.

When Macpherson saw him his hopes rose. "Couldn't I come, too?" he pleaded as Sam leapt off the cart and rushed forward to join the others.

"If there's room," Sam called back. "Come along, young fellow-me-lad. We'll see if we can fit you in. But, I'm warning you, it'll be a stormy ride. Are you sure . . . ?"

Macpherson was sure. He was off the cart and into the lifeboat in an instant, huddling down beside Mungo, hardly believing his luck. Someone handed him a life-jacket, the engine revved up, the skipper shouted an order, and before Macpherson had time to realize what was happening, the boat began to slide forward, down the runway into the sea.

The lifeboat was launched and he was in it!

9

The Final Fling

"Look, a flare! Out beyond the lighthouse. Someone signalling!" shouted Sam Thrums as the lifeboat pitched and tossed across the stormy sea. "Straight ahead, lads."

He was a different man now. No jokes, no rousing songs, no light-hearted chatter. This was not the time to waste words when lives were at stake.

Excited though he was, Macpherson had little chance to notice all that was happening. All his efforts were concentrated on keeping on an even keel. The up-and-down motion of the lifeboat was doing strange things to his stomach. Rowing with Grandpa in an oary-boat was plain sailing. But he had never experienced such a tossing and tumbling as this. At any moment it seemed as if the lifeboat would keel over and they would all be pitched overboard.

Mungo, the donkey-boy, did not seem to be turning a hair. He had flasks of hot drinks and a first-aid box beside him. "Hang on," he said to Macpherson, helping him into the life-jacket.

You'll be O.K. Look! There's the lighthouse just ahead."

By the time Macpherson had struggled into the jacket they were already passing the lighthouse. For a moment he wished he could step out and join Big Davy and Joe in their cosy living-room, with the kettle on the boil and fresh pancakes for tea. But this was no time for weakness. He took a grip of himself, clung on, and tried to ignore the heaving of the boat and of his stomach.

Suddenly the lifeboat swerved to one side and Sam Thrums called, "Man overboard! Throw out a life-belt."

Macpherson was dimly aware of a fishing-vessel listing on its side, of men shouting "Ahoy!" of the lifeboat slowing down, of strong arms stretching out to haul in a man, and of Mungo cradling him in his arms as he tried to make him drink from one of the flasks.

Could it really be happening? It was like one of Grandpa's stories or a scene from a film. The fisherman was spluttering and coughing, but soon the colour came back to his cheeks and he muttered, "Thanks, please," as Mungo offered him another drink.

"Is he foreign?" asked Macpherson, helping to support the man as he tried to sit up.

"From Brittany, I think," said Mungo, wrapping a blanket round the shivering fisherman's shoulders. "Look! Their boat's keeling over. We'll have to get the other men off."

It was a tight squeeze by the time they were all in. Four dark-skinned men, exhausted by their efforts to keep their fishing-boat from foundering. Macpherson helped to revive them with hot drinks, thankful to have something useful to do during the rough journey back to shore. They could speak little English beyond, "Is good! Thanks, please!" But what did words matter?

They were alive, and grateful to be in such good hands.

"Well, young fellow-me-lad, you've been through everything, now!" said Sam Thrums to Macpherson when the men had been helped into the coast-guard station. "What did you think of it, then?"

"Great!" said Macpherson, staggering a little as he tried to find his land legs. But he was not sure. It had all been too quick. He would have liked to do it all over again in slow motion to make certain that it had really happened. He would go home and tell Grandpa about it. That would be the best part of the adventure.

"I'm tho thad!" said Maisie Murphy, heaving a great sigh. "It'th your latht day, Macpherthon."

So it was. The last day of the holiday. How quickly it had flown.

At first Macpherson had thought the fortnight would go on for ever. Long days stretching ahead, to be filled with one glorious adventure after another. Yet here they were, packing up already to go home to Glasgow. Except Maisie and the Murphy brood, who were staying for one more week.

"What'll I do without you?" she wailed, as if she would never see him again, with great tears beginning to roll down her cheeks.

"Don't be silly," scoffed Macpherson. "I'll see you next week. In Glasgow."

But he, too, sighed; for Glasgow meant hustle and bustle, Old Skinflint shouting at him. No sea breezes, no leisure, no lighthouse.

"Cheer up, my old shipmate," said Grandpa in his hopeful manner. "Nothing wrong with Glasgow. Heaps of adventures waiting for you there. Places don't matter; it's people who are important."

Macpherson gave him a fond look. How lucky he was to have Grandpa with his cheerful outlook and understanding ways. Of course, the old man was right. What did it matter where they were as long as they were together? And, true enough, adventures could happen as easily in Glasgow as at the seaside.

Aunt Janet was not feeling so cheerful. "What's all this rubbish? You're not going to take that home with you," she said sharply to Macpherson, who was gathering together a heap of shells and seaweed which he had collected from the shore. His treasure-trove.

"It's not rubbish," he protested. "Look, Aunt Janet, some of the shells are beauties. They'll look lovely on the mantelpiece at home. And if you hold them close to your ear you can hear the sea."

"Nonsense!"

"What's wrong with a little nonsense?" said

Grandpa, backing him up. "Let the boy take them, Janet woman. They'll remind us of our holiday. The best we've ever had. Don't you agree?"

But Aunt Janet was not in an agreeable mood. She would not admit that the holiday had been a success. Certainly she was looking better, with more colour in her cheeks; but her frown was still there, and not a hint of a smile on her lips. Looking at her now, Macpherson found it difficult to imagine her singing "like a linty" in Sam Thrums's junk-cart.

He was coming later to take them all to the station. Maybe Aunt Janet would brighten up then. Maybe she, too, was feeling down-hearted at leaving Sea View.

Certainly it had not been easy for Macpherson to say goodbye to the seaside and all his new friends. Yesterday, with the sun once more beaming brightly, he had made the most of his last day of freedom. He had built the biggest sand-castle on the shore, more like a lighthouse than a castle. He had floated in the sea, gazing up at the blue sky. "I'll go more often to the baths in Glasgow and learn to swim properly," he decided. He had ridden Silly-Willy, visited Lord Ronald in the Cottage Hospital and the Duchess at the Beach Hotel. And he had called in to see the cheerful grocer at the local store.

"Help yourself to an apple and one of these

juicy oranges. Be sure to come back if you ever need a job. I could do with a smart lad like you."

If only Mr McGlashan was as generous!

He had driven Soapsuds around the country lanes, and finally pushed Grandpa's wheel-chair down to the promenade so that the old man could take a last look at the sea.

Grandpa let him gaze through his telescope. A seagull circling in the air seemed as big as an aeroplane. Then Macpherson saw the lighthouse, so near that he could almost touch it.

Suddenly, as he trained the telescope along the promenade, he saw an enlarged vision of Maisie Murphy coming into view. She was trundling the battered old pram in front of her. The baby, looking big and bouncy, was sitting up repeating the only word she knew. "Goo! Goo!"

"Goo-goo to you!" Grandpa greeted her, and began shoogling Cinderella backwards and forwards in her pram. "Leave her with me, Maisie, my dear, and go off and enjoy yourself."

"Oh, thankth, Grandpa." Maisie rewarded him with one of her smacking kisses and turned hopefully to Macpherson. "Are you coming to play, Macpherthon?"

"No, I'm not," said Macpherson bluntly. "I'm going to look for sea-shells. You can help, if you like, but keep quiet."

For a time Maisie helped, hunting amongst the

rocks for little curly shells. But she could not keep quiet. Her tongue wagged on and on. "Oh, look at thith one, Macpherthon. Ithn't it lovely? And here'th another. Let me thee what you've found."

Macpherson was so used to her non-stop chatter that he had long ago learnt not to listen. It was only after a long spell of silence that he suddenly realized Maisie was missing. She had left a little heap of shells beside him, but she herself had vanished.

"What is she up to now, the silly wee thing?" he thought impatiently, and went in search of her.

She was not with the donkey-boys, she had not gone paddling in the sea, and she had not gone back to Grandpa and Cinderella. So where could she be?

Suddenly Macpherson heard the sound of music and laughter. Along near the pier, where the Seaside Follies sometimes gave an open-air performance, a crowd had gathered to watch a Talent Competition. Someone was singing and dancing on the makeshift stage. Maisie Murphy! Holding up her trailing skirt she was twirling round and round, singing in her high-pitched voice: "I belong to Glasgow".

Her face was flushed, her hair tousled, her hat with its artificial flower on the brim almost falling off her head. But she danced and sang with such verve that the audience took her to their hearts.

At the end they clapped so loudly that the judges were unanimous in declaring her the winner.

"First prize, Miss Maisie Murphy from Glasgow."

To her delight, she was handed a large box of chocolates tied up with pink ribbon. No wonder Maisie was all smiles and bows. She was in the seventh heaven.

But that was yesterday. Today the chocolate box was empty. Maisie had shared the contents with everyone from Cinderella to Silly-Willy, and now there was only the pink ribbon left. She had tied it round her hair so that she would look her best when she waved Macpherson goodbye at the station. But her face was still tear-stained when Sam Thrums came jolting along to pick them up.

He took one look at her and said, "Cheer up, Miss Murphy, and turn off the water-works. Think how lucky you are. You'll have me and Soapsuds entirely at your service once we get rid of that lot. You can come out with me every day, if you like, rain or shine."

"Oh thankth, Mr Thrumth," said Maisie, cheering up at once. "Can I come and thit bethide you?"

Sam Thrums shook his head. "Not today, Miss Murphy. The place is reserved for another lady." He held out a helping hand to Aunt Janet. "Come along, m'dear, and keep me company."

Aunt Janet coloured, but she allowed herself to be hoisted up, and sat close beside him all the way to the station.

"Heave ho, my hearty!" called Grandpa from the back. "Take a deep breath, Macpherson, and a last look at the sea. Then we'll look forward instead. To all the fun we're going to have in Glasgow."

Macpherson was watching the lighthouse till it faded from his sight. He felt bereft when it had gone, but he had the little replica in his pocket to remind him of it. And Grandpa was right. It was best to look forward.